To Sherri,

I wish you all the best, and I hope you enjoy the book!

Nancy Hann Skroko

10-18-14

Live for Tomorrow

Nancy Hann Skroko

InspiringVoices®
A Service of **Guideposts**

Inspiring Voices books may be ordered through booksellers or by contacting:

Inspiring Voices
1663 Liberty Drive
Bloomington, IN 47403
www.inspiringvoices.com
1-(866) 697-5313

Cover Art © 2013 Howard David Johnson

ISBN: 978-1-4624-0535-0 (sc)
ISBN: 978-1-4624-0536-7 (e)

Library of Congress Control: 2013902803

Printed in the United States of America

Inspiring Voices rev. date: 04/22/2013

This novel is dedicated to God, our Heavenly Father, who makes all things possible and from whom all blessings flow, and to Jesus Christ, our Lord and Savior.

I am so thankful for my grandmother, Nana, (Ella Conterweitis Winkler Klauka), whose fascinating recollections of her life gave me the inspiration to write this book.

I am so blessed that my wonderful husband, David, and son, Mark, gave me their love and encouragement. Their faith kept me going.

I give thanks for the devotion of my beloved golden retrievers, Brandy, Sarah, and Holly; and our kitty, Miss Libby. They faithfully kept me company whenever I sat down to write.

I also thank Ruth Harley, my instructor at the Institute of Children's Literature, who in 1986-88 guided me through the completion of the first draft of this novel.

Finally, many thanks to Andrew Laverghetta and Lifetouch Photography for my portrait on the back cover of this book; to Jim Seeman for his invaluable knowledge of trains and transportation; and to Howard David Johnson, the gifted cover artist who designed the stunningly beautiful cover of my book. The cover is perfect!

Inspiring Voices Publishers, thank you for your expertise in putting this book together. You did a wonderful job!

Blessings to you all!

Chapter 1

IT WAS TWO DAYS BEFORE *Weihnachten*, 1917, and the ancient, narrow brick alleys of the imperial medieval city where the emperor Charlemagne had once ruled in Aachen, Germany, were crowded with last-minute shoppers, horse-drawn carriages, and an occasional auto. The stalwart citizens of Aachen seemed determined to enjoy the Christmas festivities despite the war, twenty-one-year-old Karina Winkler decided as she returned yet another cheerful holiday greeting from a warmly dressed passerby. She glanced at the bronze-cast figure of Charlemagne that dominated a large fountain in the middle of the cobblestone-paved market square, around which were clustered the beautifully decorated shops. Goods were displayed invitingly in the festively decorated shop windows. Karina paused momentarily in front of a tempting *konditorei* window where delectable pastries and bars of marzipan beckoned invitingly. Delicacies such as these were rare indeed due to food shortages, but the shopkeepers had saved their best for this holiest of holidays. She stared longingly at the chocolate-covered pieces of marzipan, which would taste exquisite and help ease the sting of the bitter cold, but the cost was equal to almost one week's wages. Fighting temptation, Karina reached into her satchel for some pennies, but then, reminding herself of her sacrifice to the soldiers, she turned resolutely away. She could not in good conscience enjoy such a sinfully delicious piece of confectionery while young men were starving and living in frigid foxholes while fighting to protect her country. Hunching her slender shoulders against the biting cold, she looked up in trepidation at the heavy, lead-colored clouds. She could smell the promise of snow in the air and thought that if she did not enjoy walking so much, she would be sorely tempted to take the streetcar to escape the subzero temperatures. But Karina had dressed warmly in her stylish black wool, ankle-length coat with matching fox fur hat and mitt so she could enjoy watching the crowds of shoppers, especially the young and handsome soldiers who smiled and winked as she walked by. She loved the attention and realized without the slightest bit of conceit that she was attractive enough to turn heads with her thick, long, golden-blonde waves and delicately pink cheeks contrasting strikingly with her large dark-brown eyes and long, sooty lashes.

"Karina, wait for me!" She turned to see Maria, her dearest friend and coworker at Braun's Haberdashery, running to catch up to her. Puffing from the exertion and sweating profusely despite the cold, Maria paused briefly to catch her breath. Looking somewhat disheveled from her run, Maria reached up to adjust her hat, which had slid to one side of her head despite the long hat pins that were entwined carefully through her long, dark mane. Pulling a daintily embroidered handkerchief from her satchel, she wiped her sweating brow with a plump, slightly shaking hand and, nodding at the contents within her purse, said, "Did you bring your gifts today?"

Karina smiled warmly and nodded as she opened her own satchel, her dark eyes sparkling impishly. "Yes, Maria, I did, and look, I have even wrapped them in festive paper!" Both girls admired their handiwork for a few moments until they heard a clock chime in the distance. It was time to leave, or they would be late for work. They made their way to an ancient stone overpass that looked down onto a street where soldiers had to pass on their way to the battlefields. Reaching quickly into their satchels, Karina and Maria dropped their gifts to the soldiers marching on the street below. Several of the men looked up and waved their thanks.

Nodding with satisfaction to Maria, Karina said, "Now we have made someone happy." Both girls had been saving up their salaries for months to purchase the supplies needed to make their gifts, and they had been working feverishly to complete their gifts in time for *Weihnachten*. Their gifts were hand-knit crosses, which hung from a narrow braided rope to be worn around a soldier's neck. Karina knew that Jesus was definitely needed in the trenches, and their gifts were a reminder of His constant presence. They had managed to knit over two hundred crosses, which was a small amount considering the total number of soldiers. It was a small gesture but from the heart, and Karina and Maria knew their gifts would help ease the loneliness the soldiers were feeling during this normally festive time of year. Separated from their loved ones and forced to exist in horrid conditions, the crosses would comfort and provide protection to their brave soldiers. The historical city of Aachen was the last German town before the converging borders of Germany, Belgium, and the Netherlands, so their beloved city was the final glimpse of home for the departing troops.

Sometimes Karina wondered if the war would ever end, along with the endless rationing and unrelenting thud of artillery. The front line running through Belgium was about 240 kilometers away, but the tremendous noise caused by the artillery and mines exploding was so intense that the faint but unmistakable thuds could be heard in Aachen. The sound was forever etched into Karina's subconscious mind even though she shut her eyes and tried to pretend that the forceful thuds were rumblings of thunder signaling a refreshing summer storm, and the war was a bad dream. But the illusion faded as soon as she opened her eyes. There was also no respite from the war at Braun's Haberdashery. Her employer, Herr Braun, had requested that his employees sew hospital gowns for the wounded whenever business was slow in the store. Herr Braun would deliver their gowns to the hospital weekly, and he always returned with the somber request to bring as many more gowns as they could possibly provide. Despite the fact that the haberdashery store's clientele consisted primarily of wealthy upper-class gentlemen and the nobility who still had operas to attend and social obligations to fulfill, where proper attire was mandatory, the sad truth was that the majority of the men were away at war. A soldier would occasionally venture into the haberdashery, but this was a rare occurrence. Herr Braun always insisted that the soldier accompany him upstairs to his flat to enjoy a glass of wine with a pastry. Karina dreaded these visits, for she could see the look of pain and anguish on her employer's kind face, and she knew that he was grieving for his only son, who had been killed in the war just months before. But today, despite numerous holiday shoppers, Karina found her mind wandering back to yesterday and a somewhat disturbing conversation she had with her mother regarding love and marriage.

"If you continue to work at Herr Braun's Haberdashery, Karina, someday you will find a wealthy husband," her lovely mother had said with conviction.

"Oh, Mother, he need not be wealthy," Karina had protested heatedly. "When I marry it will be for love, not wealth!"

"You are a beautiful girl, Karina, and any man would be lucky to have you for his wife," Frau Winkler had admonished gently, "but I understand why you feel as you do."

Karina had nodded miserably, acutely aware of the awkward situation in which she and her siblings found themselves. Their father, Rolf Winkler, was a handsome, wealthy man who appeared years younger than his actual age. He was the owner of a prosperous stove company, and his job required him to travel extensively. Sometimes he was away from home for months at a time. His travels took him to all parts of the world, and he always returned from his journeys with expensive and unique gifts for his wife and children. His most recent journey had been to Africa, and he had returned with an exquisitely carved ivory necklace for his wife and dainty ivory fans for Karina and her two sisters. For Karina's only brother, Adolph, Rolf Winkler had given him a Zulu warrior's spear. He also had shipped a Bengal tiger rug, made from a tiger that he himself had killed while on a hunting expedition. Karina adored her parents, but she knew that her father's long absences were the cause of enormous tension between her parents. Perhaps that was why they slept in separate bedrooms when Rolf Winkler was at home. But despite this, Karina found herself unable to accept what her mother had long suspected and recently confirmed just two months ago with the help of a private detective: her father had a *geliebte*.

"A mistress! Mother, are you sure?" Karina felt sick inside. She had recoiled in horror at the nauseating word and had nightmares imagining her handsome father lying in the sinful woman's arms while her poor mother cried herself to sleep every night.

Frau Winkler, however, had been adamant of her suspicions. After all, she had proof.

"Our marriage was arranged by our parents, as are most upper-class marriages," her mother had said. "Your father and I grew up together, and we saw each other often since our parents were close friends. I think they decided when we were both still babies that we would someday marry. A marriage contract was drawn up between our families when I was thirteen years old and your father was sixteen years of age. Even though I had no choice in the matter, I was so proud knowing that someday I would be Frau Rolf Winkler. After all, your father is an extremely attractive man and wealthy also. He was always courteous and attentive to me, but he never lacked for female companionship. He enjoyed being surrounded by attractive women, and because of his good looks, wealth, and charm, he was never disappointed."

"But Mother," Karina had protested heatedly, "you are so beautiful … how could Father do such a thing!" And it was true. Elizabeth Winkler was lovely both inside and out. Karina could not understand how her father could prefer the charms of a *geliebte* over the obvious beauty and devotion of her beloved mother.

"Yes, well, that never seemed to be enough for your father," Frau Winkler commented sadly. "Younger, more beautiful women are not hard to find, especially if one is looking. I knew that your father did not go on his business trips alone. I have known that for a long time."

Karina stood still for a long moment, feeling guilty over something she had no control over as she realized that her mother had never been able to accompany her father on his business trips because of having to care for her and her siblings. If her mother had insisted, Karina knew that they could have well afforded a nanny to care for them in her parents' absence, but her mother would have none of it. Her deep love for her children had ruined her marriage. Karina hopelessly tried to sort out her confusion as her daydream ended. She loved her parents dearly, but the friction between them was heartbreaking and sometimes more than she could bear.

"Fraulein Winkler, this gentleman would like to purchase a top hat."

Startled by a gentle tap on her shoulder, Karina glanced from the kindly face of Herr Braun into one of the most handsome faces she had ever seen. His raw virility, most noticeably evident, caused her heart to triple its beat and made her acutely aware of the gentleman's tantalizing nearness. He was young, perhaps twenty-six or twenty-seven, and very tall, well over six feet. His face was lean with a long, finely chiseled nose and a strong, masculine jawline. His firmly molded mouth suggested strength but also tenderness. He obviously enjoyed the outdoors, for he still had a tan that complemented his brown, wavy hair and dark, expressive eyes. Karina found herself gazing into their alluring depths, where she noted a hint of amusement. Smoothing her apron primly, she finally managed to utter a polite, "May I help you?" as her gaze lingered on his sensuous and masculine face.

"Yes, Fraulein." His voice was deep and confident and spoke of breeding and education. Holding up a once elegant but now crumpled top hat, he said, "I wish to purchase another one of these since my chauffeur ran over this one with the auto."

Barely able to suppress a giggle but not daring to offend her handsome customer, Karina managed to compose herself and say, "Oh, sir, I am so sorry that happened. Did you reprimand your chauffeur?"

The hint of amusement that Karina had noted earlier in the man's dark eyes now burst into warm flickers of genuine humor as he smiled broadly and laughingly shook his head. "No, Fraulein," he confirmed with mock dismay, "Hans has been with our family for as long as I can remember, and actually it was no one's fault. I came outside just as Hans was bringing the auto around to the front door. It was a blustery day, and the wind blew my top hat off directly into the auto's path. It was unavoidable."

Karina smiled inwardly. She could just imagine this obviously wealthy and extremely attractive gentleman running to retrieve his top hat. Judging from his words and actions, he seemed to be quite attached to his chauffeur and most likely dismissed the matter as a minor inconvenience. She found herself even more attracted to him because of this. She looked at the crumpled hat once more and said, "Well, you most certainly are in need of a new hat. This one is definitely beyond repair." Looking inside at the leather band, she found the size and hurried to one of the floor-to-ceiling cupboards to look for his size. Finally locating one, she hurried back and handed the new top hat to the handsome gentleman for him to try on.

"This one will be fine, Fraulein," he said as he adjusted it on his head and studied his reflection in the mirror.

"Yes, it appears to be your size," Karina agreed as she critically surveyed the fit. She looked at him again and noticed for the first time that he was in uniform. "Are you home on leave?" she inquired curiously.

"Medical leave." Running his hand restlessly through his thick, wavy hair he said, "Early in November, we were involved in heavy fighting near the front, and I was shot in the chest. Luckily the bullet ricocheted off my ribs, but it broke a few in the process. I was sent to the hospital here in Aachen, but since I live here I was allowed to recuperate at home."

"How long is your leave, that is, if you do not mind my asking?" Karina said, wondering if she would ever see him again.

"I must report back to my unit before the end of January."

"You must make the most of your time and try to rest as much as possible," Karina remonstrated, unable to disguise her obvious concern. "You have suffered a serious injury which will take quite some time to heal. Has your doctor given you permission to be out like this?" Karina bit her lip in confusion and embarrassment. She had spoken far too bluntly to this handsome man. Silently she waited for his sure-to-come reprimand.

Instead she heard an amused chuckle and felt a gentle hand lift her chin so that she had no choice but to look him in the eye. "My physician is a very wise man, for he knows that a person will not regain his strength without exercise. So you see, I am merely following his orders by being out and about. In fact," he continued, "I stopped in here because I plan to attend the opera this weekend. As you know, all festivities are frowned upon due to the war, but since it is *Weihnachten*, the opera will be allowed to play. Even though I will be in uniform, my plans made me remember that I had to replace my top hat, so I decided to do it before reporting back to duty." He studied Karina's lovely face for a moment, his dark eyes sparkling with mischief as he said, "Fraulein, would you do me the honor of allowing me to escort you to the opera on Saturday evening?"

Karina felt a hot glow rising to her cheeks, and she realized with embarrassment that she was blushing. She wanted more than anything to immediately accept his offer, but she remembered her manners and murmured demurely, "Sir, I would be most honored to accompany you, but first I must obtain my mother's permission. I will ask her this evening. Oh, and what is your name? I know she will want to know that also."

"Baron Derek von Kampler II," he replied, his dark eyes glinting with pleasure. Taking her hand into his own, he kissed it lightly and said, "I agree that you must obtain your mother's permission. Please assure her that we will also have a chaperone. Hans, my chauffeur, will be driving us to the opera. May I return tomorrow morning to obtain your answer?"

Karina nodded happily.

Bowing regally, Derek said, "Then it is settled. I will see you tomorrow morning, yes?"

"Yes, I will see you tomorrow!" Karina watched as he left the store and knew without a shadow of a doubt that she would accompany him Saturday evening. Once her mother learned the details and knew there would be a chaperone, Karina knew that she would give her permission. Karina sighed happily, unable to believe her good fortune. She would never have believed that such a wonderful man existed outside of her dreams, but he did, for she was to accompany him to the opera. Life was wonderful!

Chapter 2

As Karina assisted customers with their purchases the following morning, *Heiligabend (*Christmas Eve), she found herself thinking of the baron and the opera they would attend. In fact, she could think of nothing else! She hoped that he had been serious and that he had not been amusing himself at her expense. She once again thought of the details of their first meeting and how she had been instantly attracted to the handsome soldier. It seemed incongruous that he would ever be lacking for female companionship. With his charm, wealth, and good looks, he most certainly could have his pick of the most beautiful women in Aachen, any one of which Karina knew would be extremely honored to be in his company.

"Fraulein, could you assist me, please?"

Her doubts vanished into thin air. A shiver ran down her spine as she heard the baron's deep voice. Turning, she looked up at him and smiled shyly. "I would be honored to accompany you to the opera, Baron. My mother has given her permission."

"Good! I promise you that we will have a most enjoyable evening, Fraulein Winkler, but please, you must call me Derek."

Karina blushed prettily. "And please, call me Karina."

"Karina … what a lovely name. It suits you perfectly." Derek looked at her, his dark eyes glowing in animation. "I must admit that I am most impatiently awaiting the arrival of Saturday. I have no patience whatsoever until I attain what I want, and I want to spend time with you so that we might learn more of each other. You possess a quick wit and natural charm that I find refreshing, and your beauty is unsurpassed. I selfishly await the opera so that I might have the privilege of enjoying more of your company."

"Yes, and I of yours!" Karina blushed profusely and stammered in embarrassment, "Oh, Derek, I apologize for my impertinence! Sometimes I speak before I think!" How could she be so magnetically attracted to this handsome gentleman in such a short time? She barely knew him, yet she felt that she could read every emotion that flickered in his dark eyes and every thought that entered his mind. Perhaps it was because they matched her own. She wished that she could leave work now and spend the day with this handsome soldier. In fact, she found herself wishing that she could spend all her time with him. She blushed again as she realized the boldness of her thoughts.

"Karina, you are most assuredly not impertinent," Derek said, amused, "and never apologize for a compliment." He studied her for a moment and said, "I find you completely fascinating ... one moment an innocent girl and the next a sophisticated woman of the world. Please do not ever change!" Suddenly it was Derek's turn to look confused.

Karina recognized the look instantly and said laughingly, "As you said, never apologize for a compliment!"

Derek laughed and said, "Perhaps, Karina, after the opera, you would do me the honor of accompanying me on a tour of our castle. It was built in the fourteenth century. One can still imagine knights in armor on their magnificent steeds and how it must have been all those years ago. I myself still expect to find a knight lurking somewhere in the shadows of the castle, and I have lived there my entire life. It is a fascinating place."

"Derek, I would love to see your castle, but would we have enough time after the opera? My mother would not approve of me being out late, and remember there is a curfew."

"Oh, yes, I had forgotten about the curfew," Derek replied

thoughtfully. "It might be better if I showed you the castle on Sunday instead. Then we will have the entire day. Would that be agreeable with you?"

"Wonderful!" Karina agreed immediately, dimpling prettily. She could barely conceal her joy. Instead, to hide her confusion and to appear sensible, she said, "What time does the opera begin?"

"Half past seven, so Hans and I will be at your flat promptly at six."

"This is my address," Karina said, bending down to write her address on a piece of paper. She ripped it off and handed the paper to Derek. As she did so, their hands met briefly, and Karina found the piece of paper replaced by a slim, tastefully wrapped gift that Derek had deftly slipped into her hand. She looked up in confusion and said, "What ... is this for me?"

Derek nodded and smiled, his pure white teeth contrasting strikingly against his tanned skin. "Tomorrow is *Weihnachten*, and the beginning of the three-day celebration. Please accept this small gift as a token of my esteem. Perhaps you would do me the honor of wearing it to the opera."

With shaking fingers, Karina tore the wrap from the box and opened the cover. "Derek, oh, how lovely!" she breathed, her gaze caressing the contents within, "but I cannot accept this. It is so expensive!" She looked again in the box. The inside was lined in black velvet, and on that rested a sapphire and diamond necklace with matching earrings. The sapphires were exquisite, a rich royal blue, and the diamonds were perfectly flawless, with the largest sapphires and diamonds in the middle and decreasing in size to the smallest at the ends. A single large sapphire surrounded by small sparkling diamonds decorated each earring. Karina looked up at Derek, overwhelmed. "Thank you so much," she breathed shakily, "but I cannot accept this."

"Oh, but you must, for I am looking forward to your wearing it on Saturday, Karina. I am a very wealthy man and well able to afford such items. I appreciate beauty in all its forms and immediately thought of you when I saw the necklace. Your flawless beauty will enhance its perfect symmetry. It was made for you."

Karina was standing so near to Derek that she could breathe in his scent. He smelled of spices and soap, an intoxicatingly masculine smell that made her heart pound and her senses reel so that she found herself unable to think clearly. All she knew was that she longed to be near him, and that she desperately wanted to keep the necklace and earrings. A small inner voice, however, warned her that she could not accept such a gift from a man she barely knew, for what would he expect in return, but she shrugged it off as she found herself becoming lost in the sensuousness of his dark eyes. Eyes so black that she could see herself reflected in their depths. But she could see something else too. It was recognition of her innocence and a reassurance that his intentions were honorable. Derek's eyes were a window to his soul, and Karina knew he could be trusted. Shyly she smiled and said, "Thank you again, Derek. I have never owned such an exquisite piece of jewelry, and sapphire is my birthstone. I was born in September."

"Karina, this jewelry was meant for you," Derek said approvingly. "You will look lovely wearing it on Saturday, I am sure." He glanced around the store, noticing for the first time the crowd of customers and the discreet glances of Karina's coworkers. "It looks as if I have taken up way too much of your time, Karina," Derek said apologetically. "I have been selfishly keeping you from your work."

Karina nodded reluctantly, not wanting him to leave. "I should be getting back to work, I guess." She glanced again at the jewelry case in her hand and smiled up at Derek, her cheeks slightly flushed, her dark eyes sparkling. "Thank you again for this lovely gift. I will cherish it always."

Derek bowed slightly and gently kissed her hand. *"Auf wiedersehen* and *Frohliche Weihnachten.* Until Saturday, yes?"

Karina watched his retreating figure at the window until he was lost in the crowd, and turning, smiled in disbelief at her friend Maria, who had witnessed the entire scene.

"Ach, Karina, he is so handsome!" Maria whispered enviously. "I wish he would have asked me out! He is handsome, wealthy, and a baron too!"

"I cannot believe it either," Karina agreed as she glanced once again at the lovely jewelry and realized that the proof lay in her hands.

Karina awoke the following morning, *Weihnachten*, in a state of anticipation. There was so much to look forward to, she thought, as she hurried to dress and join her family in the many holiday festivities.

"Karina, where have you been?" her youngest sister, Gertrude, demanded impatiently, jumping up and down in excitement. "You know that Mama will not allow us into the parlor until we are all here!"

Karina smiled apologetically at Gertrude and her other sister, Minna, and her brother, Adolph, who jumped guiltily away from the parlor doors, where he had been trying to catch a glimpse of the room within through the small space separating the two panels. At fifteen years of age, Adolph was the second oldest sibling and the man of the house in his father's absence.

"Is Mother ready for us yet?" Karina inquired, eager herself to open her gifts. Packages had been arriving almost daily for the past several weeks, gifts from their father who was too far away to make it home in time for *Weihnachten*.

Suddenly they heard the key turn in the lock, and Frau Winkler pushed open the parlor doors to reveal a large pine tree glowing softly with lighted candles in the center of the room. In keeping with family tradition, the tree was heavily laden with cookie ornaments and chocolate and marzipan candies, and the gifts fanned out from beneath making a huge and gaily colored tree skirt. Karina felt a momentary stab of pain at the absence of their father, who always led the family in the singing of Yuletide carols before the opening of gifts, but she noticed the lack of tension in her mother's beautiful face and knew it was for the best. Despite Rolf Winkler's infidelity, or perhaps because of it, he lavished gifts upon his wife, sparing no expense in providing her with the finest. He was equally generous with his children, but Karina would gladly have traded it all in exchange for a happy family life. The rift between her parents had left an emotional scar that no amount of presents could erase. Despite the momentary sadness, Karina felt her spirits lift, as *Weihnachten* was a happy time, and she was determined to enjoy the day.

Due to their father's absence, the family's holiday ritual was altered a bit, with Adolph leading them in the carol singing, his deep baritone mingling richly with the delicate sopranos of his mother and sisters. Since Herr Winkler usually passed out the gifts, Adolph did that too.

"Oh, look," Karina whispered, her chocolate-brown eyes glistening with tears as she gently stroked the white mink muff and hat that her father had sent from Russia. She glanced up in time to see her mother lift the cover off a huge box and take out a note that was lying on top of the tissue paper.

"Girls, listen," Frau Winkler said as she quickly scanned the note, "your father has sent several bolts of velvet ... enough to make a new dress for each us!" Tearing the tissue paper open, she carefully lifted several bolts out of the box for them to admire.

Karina fingered the soft cloth lovingly and tried to decide which color she would choose for herself. It would be a difficult decision as she glanced indecisively from the rich royal blue to the crimson red bolts and to the equally lovely deep purple and emerald green colors. A new dress in the midst of war was a luxury indeed! The family finished opening the rest of the gifts and then sat down to a scrumptious breakfast of oatmeal, baking powder biscuits, and warm cinnamon coffeecake. Frau Winkler had been saving up every measure of food in order to prepare some of the delicacies they usually enjoyed at this time of year, and had paid dearly for these items on the black market. After breakfast they attended *Weihnachten* Mass at the cathedral. The ancient church looked lovely decorated with fresh pine boughs and softly glowing candles, and as the congregation sang the precious carols, the mood was somber despite the holiness of the day. After Mass, Karina and her family decided to walk the several blocks to their grandparents, where the house was crowded with jovial aunts, uncles, and cousins. The children could barely sit still long enough to enjoy the scrumptious dinner of chicken, stuffing, mashed potatoes and gravy, and several delectable desserts in their eagerness to escape outside for sled riding and ice skating. Karina's two younger sisters considered the outdoor activities too unladylike, but Karina loved the competition and happily joined in the fun. As she jumped on a sled, she lost her grip and tumbled into the soft snow. She lay there for a moment, staring up into the darkening afternoon sky, and realized happily that tomorrow at this time she would be preparing for her opera date with Derek. Smiling wryly, she realized that she was a woman of contrasts as Derek had noted, and she wondered if he would be surprised at this tomboy side of her. Because of the three-day *Weihnachten* holiday, she would have all day tomorrow to prepare for her outing and the entire day after that to spend with Derek at his castle.

The following evening after surveying herself in the mirror, Karina thought that she had never looked lovelier. She had piled her thick blonde hair into a becoming upsweep that added inches to her petite stature and accentuated her long, slender neck. Her opera outfit was a birthday gift from her father and had been made in Paris. The delicate blouse was made of three layers of sheer light sapphire blue chiffon. Tiny blue rosebuds were embroidered on the open collar, front placket, and French cuffs with delicate mosaic buttons imported from Italy completing the blouse. The floor-length satin skirt was a deep sapphire blue with a matching cummerbund that accentuated her tiny twenty-inch waist to its best advantage.

Dainty blue satin slippers peeked demurely from beneath the skirt. Blue was Karina's favorite color and was one in which she looked particularly lovely. She picked up a crystal decanter from her dresser and dabbed another drop of rosewater behind each ear. All she had left to do was put on Derek's sapphire and diamond necklace and earrings. She carefully opened the blue velvet jewelry case and gently lifted the stunning necklace from its soft bed. Slowly she fastened the sapphire necklace around her neck and clipped the earrings on her ears and surveyed herself once again in the full-length mirror. The stunning diamonds reflected tiny prisms of light, and the beauty of the sapphires complemented the elegance of her opera attire.

"Karina, *meine kind*," her mother called gently as she tapped on the door, "are you ready? Baron von Kampler is waiting downstairs in the parlor!"

"*Danke*, Mama." Glancing one last time in the mirror, she grabbed her blue velvet cape and purse from the bed. She felt her heart beat faster at the sound of Derek's name and a flicker of nervousness, but she could hardly wait to see Derek again. She fingered the lovely sapphire necklace appreciatively, lifted her head spiritedly and went downstairs to greet her date.

He was standing before the fireplace in the guest parlor, impeccably dressed in his dress uniform and holding his hat. He looked devastatingly handsome and completely at ease, and Karina felt her heart thump madly in response to his masculinity.

Crossing the room in easy strides, Derek bowed to Karina, his dark eyes traveling approvingly over her as his eyes rested momentarily on the stunning necklace. "You look lovely, Karina. Your beauty brings out the best in the necklace and earrings."

"Thank you, Derek, you are too kind," Karina murmured demurely as she felt herself blushing at his undisguised admiration, "You have met my mother, yes?"

"Yes, Karina, I have," Derek agreed as he turned and smiled admiringly at Karina's mother. "And now that I have had the honor of meeting you, Frau Winkler, may I say that I see where Karina has inherited her beauty. The resemblance is unmistakable."

Frau Winkler blushed and smiled appreciatively at his compliment. "Thank you so much, Baron von Kampler, for your kindness. May I inquire as to the health of the baron and baroness?"

"Mother is well, but Father is still bedridden and will be for the rest of his life, I am afraid. The accident has put a severe strain on his heart."

"*Ach*, such a sad thing to have happened," Frau Winkler nodded sympathetically. "I remember reading of the accident in the paper. Your father is still such a young man. It must be a difficult adjustment for him."

Derek nodded sadly. "It has been very difficult for him, but he tries to keep busy and still manages to run the estate."

Karina nodded in sympathy, her heart going out to Derek's father. Karina had overheard the girls at Braun's Haberdashery speaking of Derek and his family, and even though Karina did her best not to listen, she had heard snatches of their conversation mentioning the baron and a horrible accident; but she felt it impolite to eavesdrop, so she did not know the details of the accident.

Not wanting to increase Derek's obvious anguish, Karina decided it best not to ask him what had happened. She realized that her mother must feel the same way, for she walked over to Derek and put her arm around his shoulders, almost as if comforting a small child, and gave him a reassuring hug.

"Do not give up hope that your father will recover, Derek," Frau Winkler said, tears evident in her gentle eyes, "It is sometimes amazing what rest and the proper nutrition can accomplish."

Derek nodded sadly, his dark eyes meeting Karina's for a brief moment before he took Karina's cloak and draped it carefully around her slender shoulders. Turning once again to Frau Winkler, he said, "We should be going so that we are not late. My chauffeur is waiting downstairs with the auto."

Frau Winkler smiled gently and shook Derek's extended hand. "It is so good to meet you, Baron. Have a wonderful evening."

Karina smiled reassuringly at her mother as she gave her a quick hug before Derek closed the door behind them. Her enchanted evening was about to begin, and Karina felt wonderfully alive and deliciously excited. She glanced up at the handsome man at her side and hoped he felt the same. Karina had seen the look of worry in Derek's eyes when Frau Winkler mentioned his father, and Karina vowed silently to be especially attentive to help him forget his pain.

It was bitterly cold and snowing lightly as Derek guided Karina into the auto's elegant leather interior. Picking up a woolen blanket, Derek tucked it securely around them, making sure to cover their feet to keep out the cold. Glancing at the luxurious surroundings, Karina snuggled appreciatively deeper under the heavy robe and said to Derek, "This is the first time I have ridden in an auto and the first time I have gone out with a man." Horrified, Karina clapped her gloved hand over her mouth and added hastily, her cheeks burning despite the cold, "What … what I meant to say is that I have always dated boys my own age who seemed too nervous to even speak to me." Never had she dated anyone as charming and sophisticated as Derek.

Derek chuckled easily and moved slightly closer to Karina, so close in fact that Karina could clearly smell the spicy aroma of his cologne. His dark eyes sparkled with amusement as he said, "I find that I never know what you will say next, my lovely fraulein, and I find that utterly charming!" Stretching his long legs, Derek said lazily, "In response to your first statement, this is a nice auto but only in the city. Once out of town and on rutted dirt roads, it is quite an inconvenience. Poor Hans, I am afraid, has had to change many a flat tire."

Karina glanced skeptically at the elderly chauffeur. He looked much too frail to be able to handle such physical exertion. Karina suspected that Derek changed the flat tires while Hans supervised.

"And as for your last statement," Derek replied easily, his ebony eyes glowing warmly, "I am a man, and I am neither nervous or shy, and I am very, very interested in you." An electric charge raced through the auto's elegant interior as both realized the depth of their attraction, so neither one noticed that the auto had reached its destination of the opera house until Hans awkwardly cleared his throat.

Karina tore her gaze away from Derek's long enough to see that they had stopped directly in front of Aachen's opera house, which had been built to look like a Roman temple. Built entirely of white Italian marble, it glowed elegantly in the gathering dusk and softly falling snow. Accepting Derek's outstretched hand, they walked up the white marble steps and between the huge columns gracing the entrance into the richly appointed foyer. Once inside, an usher greeted Derek respectfully and escorted them to a private box to the right of the stage. Settling herself carefully into the plush velvet seat, Karina sensed that she was being stared at, and holding her head high, she knew it was because she was with Derek. He was obviously well-known and respected. Despite his tantalizing nearness, Karina found her attention riveted to the stage as the opera began. At intermission, Derek escorted her downstairs to enjoy refreshments and mingle with other patrons. Derek knew most of them, and Karina noted that he seemed to be taking a great deal of pleasure in introducing her to his friends. They returned to their seats for the second half of the opera, and almost before she knew it, the opera had ended and Derek was escorting her to the waiting auto.

"Did you enjoy it?" Derek asked as they settled themselves into the auto's soft seats.

"Oh, it was wonderful!" Karina enthused, her eyes still slightly misty and soft. The ending had been sad but very romantic.

"I enjoyed it also," Derek agreed, "especially when I am with such an enchanting companion."

"Everyone seemed to know you, Derek. I felt that we were being stared at when we found our seats."

"Ah, my dear Karina, it was not *me* they were staring at, but rather *you*. The men were admiring your flawless beauty while their wives were making note of who I was with so they could gossip about it at the next social function. Nothing escapes their sharp eyes, I am sure." Derek glanced over at Hans, who was waiting patiently for further orders. "Karina, now we will have something to eat, yes? Hans, take us to the Goldener Schwan." The Goldener Schwan was a small pub located across from Charlemagne's golden statue in the marketplace and just around the corner from Braun's Haberdashery.

As they entered the dark, cozy interior, a jovial, plump man with thick glasses and balding head came running to greet them, his arms outstretched in greeting.

"Ah, Baron von Kampler, it is good to see you again!" he said, vigorously shaking Derek's hand. "Shall I give you your usual booth?"

"Yes, Herr Schwartz, that would be good," Derek said as the man led them to an intimate corner.

"Would you prefer to see menus, or would you like tonight's special?" Herr Schwartz inquired attentively as he quickly poured them steaming mugs of coffee. "The special this evening is chicken dumpling soup, potato pancakes with sausages and applesauce, and chocolate cake or apple strudel for dessert."

"Karina?"

"I would like the special, if that meets with your approval, Derek."

Derek nodded at Herr Schwartz. "Yes, please bring us both the special and also a bottle of red wine."

"I will have Helga bring it immediately." Herr Schwartz bowed briefly and disappeared into the kitchen. Shortly thereafter a tall, dark-haired woman appeared carrying the wine with two glasses.

"Ah, Baron von Kampler, it is good to see you ..." Helga murmured politely as she poured their wine, her eyes glancing curiously at Karina.

"And so good to see you again, Frau Schwartz," Derek said. "May I introduce to you my lovely companion, Fraulein Karina Winkler. We have just been to the opera, and we are eagerly awaiting one of your delicious entrees."

Once again Karina felt Frau Schwartz's curious gaze upon her as both women exchanged a polite greeting.

"Enjoy your wine," Helga said brightly, "and your meal will be ready shortly."

Karina relaxed against the upholstered bench and savored her glass of wine, the warmth from it banishing any remaining chills. Looking shyly at Derek she said, "I have had such a wonderful evening. The opera, your company … I cannot ever remember having had such a superb evening. I never want it to end!"

Reaching across the table and capturing Karina's small hand into his, Derek smiled tenderly. "Maybe it is because we are meant for each other, Karina."

Karina looked uncertainly at Derek to see if he was teasing her, but his dark, expressive eyes were sincere. Whatever she felt in her own heart, Karina knew she was a novice at love and sensed that she must control her emotions and try to listen to common sense … even though that was the last thing she wanted to do. So she said slowly, thoughtfully, "Derek, how can you be sure we are meant for each other? We have known each other such a short time."

Just then Helga appeared carrying their dinner, which she set before them carefully.

They ate in silence for a few moments as each pondered the magnitude of Karina's statement.

"Karina," Derek said finally, pausing a moment in order to organize his thoughts, "you asked how I know we are meant for each other. I find myself looking forward to any time we spend together; no other woman I have dated has ever affected me in that way. I have dated many women; they did not interest me enough to ask out for a second time, let alone entertain thoughts of marriage." Shaking his head, he said, "there was always something missing … and now that I have met you," he said, gently pulling her hand into his, "I know what that something was. They lacked your vitality, your love of life, your beguiling innocence. You, Karina, and you alone, have captured my heart as no other woman ever has or ever will."

"Oh, Derek," Karina whispered softly, her eyes filling with tears, "I … I feel the same way about you, but this is all so new to me." Her voice trailed off as she looked down at the food before her, afraid that she had hurt his feelings. Karina felt gentle hands lift her chin so that she was once again looking into Derek's dark eyes.

"I know it is," he agreed quietly, "and you are very wise for being cautious and not letting your heart overrule your head." He paused momentarily. "I once ignored this advice and suffered the most dire of consequences because of it. I vowed that I would never let that happen again."

"What happened, Derek?"

"I asked a woman to marry me."

"Oh!" Involuntarily, Karina's hand flew to the sapphire necklace encircling her throat. Suddenly it felt like a noose—Derek could pull his end if he so chose to at any time. Had she misread his intentions? Would he take advantage of her lack of experience and innocence? She forced herself to look into his eyes. Whatever she had feared to find was not there; his eyes held a faraway look, and with relief she realized that he had not noticed her reaction. "You asked a woman to marry you?" Karina prodded gently.

Derek smiled ruefully and nodded. "Yes, just once. It was a long time ago, when I was seventeen and very immature." A myriad of emotions flashed across his handsome features as his dark eyes flashed with anger. "That long-ago summer, I was invited to stay with my parents' good friends, who owned a villa in Rome. Their son, Mario, and I were the same age, and we had been friends since childhood.

Mario and I decided we wanted to live life to the fullest, so we spent our days gambling and our nights partying. At one party, Mario introduced me to a particularly stunning young woman; her name was Angelina. She had long, ebony black hair; dark, flashing eyes; and a flawless olive complexion. She was a striking beauty, so dark in a shimmery white dress, and I thought her the loveliest woman I had ever seen. She was surrounded by ardent admirers, myself included. As the party progressed into the night, and we became increasingly intoxicated, I found it harder and harder to get Angelina's attentions. My solution was to become more drunk. Finally, as the evening waned into the wee hours of early morning, I could stand it no more. I decided to ask Angelina to marry me. I was so intoxicated that I did not even think of taking her somewhere private to ask her. Instead, I pulled her into the middle of the dance floor, bowed unsteadily, and said in a slurred voice, 'I, Derek von Kampler II, son of Baron von Kampler, and heir to Castle Royale, do hereby request your lovely hand in marriage.' I had finally gotten her attention.

"Angelina stared unsteadily at me for a moment, rage building in her ebony eyes. She dropped my hand as if I were a leper and screeched, 'A *baron*! You're the son of a lowly *baron*? I would not marry you if you were the last man on earth!'

"Even in my drunken state, I could see that any further attempts to change her mind were futile, so I attempted to quietly leave the dance floor. But that, of course, was impossible since everyone in the room had witnessed my absurd marriage proposal.

"Angelina turned to the unruly crowd; she was also greatly intoxicated, and shouted loudly, 'Imagine me, Angelina Maria Libertino, daughter of the great Count Libertino, marrying a lowly baron's son!' Pointing to me scornfully she said, 'You could not even support a peasant girl, let alone royalty! Go back to Germany, you rotten, stinking idiot!' With that, she turned and stumbled self-righteously off the dance floor amidst shouts of derisive laughter."

Derek paused momentarily and then continued, "Thank *Gott* I was drunk, for it dulled my senses. I stumbled out of the room and back to Mario's villa, where I slept off my humiliation for the next two days. When I finally woke up, Mario had done some investigating and learned that, as a joke, some rival suitor had, out of jealousy, informed Angelina that I was a prince. When she found out that I indeed was not, she was furious. She was well-known for her violent temper."

Karina could stand no more. "Derek," she said, shaking her head in confusion, "how could she be so cruel?"

"Sometimes the world is a cruel place," Derek replied soberly.

Karina thought how easy it would have been for Derek to retaliate against Angelina and humiliate her instead, but he was too much of a gentleman to stoop to such behavior. Looking at the handsome, sensuous man seated across from her, she could not understand how any woman could behave like that. She said softly, "You had a terrible experience, Derek. But … have you not asked anyone else to marry you since due to her? Have you rejected the institution of marriage forever?" She was afraid to hear his answer.

"No, Karina," Derek reassured her quickly, taking her hands into his own. "What it did was teach me a valuable lesson. I vowed not to marry until I was absolutely certain that I had found my one true love. Someone whom I knew I could not live without. Someone like you … Karina, will …"

Shaking her head gently, Karina placed a slender finger on Derek's lips to gently silence him. She knew what he was going to say, and even though her heart ached for him to finish his proposal so that she could say yes, her logical self protested that love takes time and should not be rushed. Blinking back tears of joy, she smiled at Derek and said gently, "If this is real and meant to be, let us enjoy and savor this time we have together so as to learn more of each other and not rush into anything. I want to enjoy each and every moment I have with you."

Derek nodded in understanding, and the look of joy in his eyes made Karina feel weak with emotion.

It was snowing heavily when they left the pub shortly thereafter, but Karina barely noticed as she relaxed against Derek's muscular shoulder on the drive home. Gazing at Derek's handsome profile in the dim light, she murmured dreamily, "This has been such a magical evening. I feel like a princess."

"And tomorrow I will show my princess her castle," Derek replied, pulling her close. "May I call for you midmorning?"

"Yes, that would be perfect. Mama will be so thrilled to see you again."

"Perfect. Hans and I will be there." The auto pulled up slowly to the curb in front of her flat.

Suddenly Karina felt awkward. She longed for Derek to kiss her on the lips, but she knew that this was not proper behavior on a first date. She turned to Derek, intending to thank him for the lovely evening when suddenly she felt Derek's lips touch hers for the briefest second. She felt as though time had stopped, and all she could focus on was the unfamiliar electric charge racing through her body.

Derek smiled gently and said, understanding in his eyes, "Is this a first also, Karina?" Derek guided her carefully up the icy steps to the door of the darkened building. "Until tomorrow," he said, caressing her cheek tenderly.

"Yes, Derek," she breathed shakily, "until tomorrow. And … thank you for such a wonderful evening." She watched until the auto was out of sight and then sank slowly onto the stairs. All evening she had tried to be sensible, to subdue her feelings, but after Derek had kissed her, Karina knew she could not deny her feelings any longer—she was in love.

Chapter 3

SEVERAL INCHES OF NEW SNOW blanketed the ground the following morning, but Karina felt oblivious to its beauty for she worried that Derek would be unable to navigate the roads in his unpredictable auto. This meant that they would not be able to visit Castle Royale. Karina unlatched her bedroom window and pushed it open to breathe in some of the cold, invigorating air while at the same time hoping to see Derek coming up the street. Her fears were unfounded, for just then she heard the tinkling of sleigh bells on the street below and saw that it indeed was Derek. She grabbed her cape and fur mitt and called a quick good-bye to her mother as she ran eagerly down the stairs, meeting Derek at the front door. For a moment she was blinded by the sun shining on the thick blanket of new snow.

"Oh, I am so glad to see you, Derek," Karina cried jubilantly as they walked to the sleigh. "I was afraid that our excursion would be cancelled because of the snow."

"Yes, it would have been with the unreliable auto," Derek agreed as he tucked fur lap robes around them, "but not with the sleigh." He nodded to Hans, who in turn picked up the reins and clucked to the matched set of bays that pawed the snow, eager to be off. They moved slowly along the narrow streets of the city, their progress hampered by the many people out enjoying the holiday. Karina snuggled closer to Derek under the robe and felt warm and cozy despite the biting cold.

"You look lovely, Karina," Derek said admiringly. Her long hair was loose, the golden curls tumbling in profusion from beneath her white fur hat. Her cheeks were pink from the cold, and as she smiled her thanks, her perfect white teeth contrasted strikingly with the darkness of her large eyes and long lashes.

Karina felt the attraction too as she gazed at Derek's magnificent profile, his dark wavy hair glistening in the winter sun. He was dressed impeccably in his uniform and a long, woolen cape.

"Today I am proud to show you my home, Castle Royale," Derek said as they made their way through what had once been a gate in the stone wall that still surrounded Aachen and had protected it from invaders during the Middle Ages. The narrow snow-covered road led to a dense pine forest that stretched unbroken for miles. Once they reached the woods, the road narrowed to one lane as it curved back and forth to accommodate the upward climb. Soon all of Aachen was visible below. Hans pulled on the reins to halt the horses, who were breathing heavily from the exertion.

"A lovely view of our beloved city, yes?" Derek said as he gazed down at the snow-covered streets and houses. They had stopped in the clearing of a large bluff, which afforded them a view of the surrounding countryside. Derek pointed to the steep incline on the road ahead. "Once we round that curve, you will be able to view Castle Royale." Hans motioned for the horses to continue, and as they rounded the curve that Derek had pointed out, Castle Royale loomed into view.

The castle was still a mile away, but its enormous size made it appear much closer. The ancient walls of the stone castle rose majestically from a sheer cliff that allowed its occupants a commanding view of the countryside below.

"Castle Royale was built during the early Middle Ages," Derek explained to Karina, "and as you can see, much thought went into its strategic location. It was impossible for invaders to scale the sheer walls of the cliff, so my ancestors had one less side to defend in battle."

Karina looked at the ancient walls of the medieval castle and felt a shiver of apprehension run down her spine. The place looked cold and uninviting, and she was glad for Derek's protective presence. Hopefully the interior was more inviting.

They reached the entrance, a long private drive lined on both sides with old-growth pine trees that formed natural snow breaks in the winter. Hans guided the horses up the drive and stopped before two massive wooden gates. He climbed stiffly from the sleigh and walked up a short brick pathway and knocked on the door of a small stone caretaker's cottage located to the left of the road. The door was answered by a plump, white-haired man who nodded briefly and disappeared back inside the cottage. As Hans climbed back into the sleigh, the gates groaned loudly and slowly opened onto a large brick courtyard. They drove through and stopped momentarily before another set of two huge and ornately carved wooden gates that were slowly pulled open by two young stable boys. Hans stopped the horses in front of a large L-shaped building that housed the stables so the horses could be attended to. The bays tossed their heads and nickered impatiently as the stable boys unhooked the horses from their traces and led into them into the warmth and protection of the barn. To the right was a stone wall inset with a small door, which Karina guessed led to the castle. As Derek lifted her from the sleigh, Karina felt for a brief moment that she was back in the Middle Ages. She would not have been the least bit surprised to see an armor-clad knight lead his trusty steed from the dim interior of the ancient stable.

Derek must have read her thoughts for he nodded and said, "It does not look like the twentieth century here, does it?"

"This is so impressive," Karina said as she gazed at the ancient surroundings in admiration. "Imagine how many of your ancestors have lived here ... and died here also."

Derek nodded as he opened the door and guided Karina farther into the castle grounds. "This castle was built somewhere around 1300 AD, which makes it a little over six hundred years old. Much

29

of those six hundred years have been spent defending these walls from invaders. You will see proof of that in just a few moments." The doorway opened directly onto a long driveway that led to the main entrance of the castle proper. As they walked slowly up the brick path, Derek tucked Karina's hand into his own and motioned to the castle. "One thing you have noticed already, I am sure, is the massive size of the castle itself."

Karina glanced up at the intimidating ancient stone walls and felt a twinge of apprehension. The castle was enormous and appeared cold and uninviting. She was so glad that Derek was at her side, as she never would have ventured into such a place otherwise. Was it her imagination or did she sense a feeling of foreboding and gloom?

They had reached the main entrance and paused on a stone porch as Derek pulled on a thick rope hanging next to the door to summon the butler. While they waited, Derek pointed to the thick, ornately carved oak doors and said, "These were built to withstand a siege. The enemy sometimes used battering rams to break down the door to gain entrance into the castle."

Karina ran her fingers over deep grooves etched in the wood. "What are these from?"

"Legend has it that once invading barbarians broke through the line of soldiers defending the castle walls and began hacking at these doors with axes."

"Did they succeed in breaking in?"

"No. Look." Derek pointed upwards to two towers located on either side of the entrance. "My ancestors stood in those towers and poured boiling oil down onto the invaders and then ignited it with flaming arrows. The men were literally cooked inside their armor." He paused. "It sounds brutal, I know, but the invaders would have been equally as cruel if they had gained access into the castle."

Karina shuddered. She did not want to think of what horrible fate the occupants of the castle would have suffered at the hands of the invaders. It was a wonderful winter day, and she was beside herself with joy at the prospect of spending the entire day with the man she loved.

The door was opened by an elderly white-haired butler, and they entered into what appeared to be a huge banquet hall. Two enormous walk-in stone fireplaces dominated the entire left side of the room. Each fireplace was large enough to accommodate the roasting of three deer or cattle simultaneously on long iron spits. At the moment, a roaring fire was burning in one fireplace, which made the room feel wonderfully warm after their long walk outdoors. The walls and floor were gray stone, and the floor was worn smooth in spots from centuries of foot traffic. The room would have been dreary and dismal if not for tasteful decorating. Colorful oriental carpets were placed throughout the room, and elegant red velvet draperies hung at the three long, narrow windows carved into the wall opposite the fireplaces. Several tapestries depicting long-ago battle scenes were displayed to the right of the doorway, and the family coat of arms was prominently displayed above the fireplace mantle. Derek walked over to the massive walnut dining table in the center of the spacious room and said, "Huge feasts were held here centuries ago. There used to be long rows of crude wooden tables and benches, easily enough to seat three hundred people at once." He nodded toward the fireplaces. "The fireplaces had to be large enough to roast several carcasses at once. Back then they literally had to feed an army."

Karina glanced admiringly around the large room. Despite its size, the room had an inviting, almost cozy feel to it. She mentioned this to Derek.

He nodded. "I know what you mean, and I believe it is due to the homey touches—the oriental carpets and the flowers. Mother has a greenhouse, so we are able to enjoy fresh flowers even in winter." He took her hand. "Come," he said, "I would like for you to meet my family."

Karina felt her earlier sense of apprehension returning as Derek led her down a series of long, dimly lit corridors. They passed several rooms before finally stopping in front of two elaborately carved mahogany panel doors. Derek knocked lightly and opened them onto a beautiful sitting room. The room was lavishly decorated and distinctly feminine. Deep rose-colored carpeting complemented a rose and white striped Queen Anne sofa and two matching armchairs, which were grouped cozily around a white Italian marble fireplace. Dainty pastel floral paintings were displayed throughout the room to enhance the light oak paneling. A woman was seated at the far end of the room with her back to the doorway.

"Mother," Derek called as they crossed the room, "I have someone here that I would like you to meet." At the sound of her son's voice, the woman rose gracefully and slowly walked toward them. Resting his hand lightly, almost protectively, on Karina's shoulder, Derek said, "Mother, I would like to introduce you to Fraulein Karina Winkler."

"It is an honor to meet you, Baroness von Kampler," Karina murmured and curtsied gracefully. Eager to discern the personality of Derek's mother, Karina glanced upward and found herself being coldly scrutinized by a pair of brilliant sapphire-blue eyes. The baroness was very tall and slender with thick auburn hair that curled attractively around her heart-shaped face. Her pale complexion was flawless and unlined, almost like a mask, Karina thought. She was elegantly beautiful but haughtily aristocratic.

Kissing Derek lightly on the cheek, the baroness glanced curiously at Karina. "So … this must be the little girl you have been telling me about, Derek." Taking Karina's hands into her own, she smiled warmly and said, "How nice of you to visit us, Katrina!"

"Her name is Karina, Mother," Derek corrected quickly.

"Oh, Karina it is," the baroness enunciated, laughing lightly. "I am sorry, dear." She shook her head in mock dismay. "Derek has so many girlfriends that sometimes I am unable to keep all their names straight." Turning her beautiful sapphire eyes to her son, the baroness said in a wounded voice, "You did date a Katrina not too long ago, didn't you, dear? Wasn't she Baron von Richter's lovely daughter?"

"Yes," Derek replied in exasperation, "I probably did date a Katrina at one time, Mother, but I do not remember a thing about her since you have introduced me to every female of marriageable age from your vast collection of friends and acquaintances!"

"Well, dear, it is only because I want you to marry someone suitable to our social position," the baroness replied innocently as she glanced meaningfully in Karina's direction. Laying her hand lightly on Karina's arm she said, "Derek told me the amusing story of how you helped him purchase another top hat. Wasn't he a gentleman to ask you to the opera?"

"Yes, Baroness, Derek is a gentleman," Karina agreed easily, thinking that all his good qualities must have been inherited from his father. She held out her hand. "It was a pleasure to meet you, Baroness von Kampler." With that, she turned her back on the Baroness. Karina did not care if she was being rude. She felt confused and more than a little angry. She had been ready to believe the warm smile on the Baroness's lips, but it had been overruled by the cold and calculating look in her sapphire eyes. Karina knew that this woman did not like her and could not be trusted. As she began to walk away, the baroness once again laid a hand on her arm.

"Please, Katrina, do not leave so quickly," the baroness said sweetly. "We have only just met, and I am interested in you. Where is your estate, dear?"

Again Karina saw the sweet smile betrayed by the mocking eyes. This rude woman is trying to embarrass me, Karina realized angrily. She thinks that I am not good enough for her son. Taking a deep breath to steady her nerves Karina replied, "Our summer home is in Switzerland, in the Alps. In Aachen, we live in a flat." Her irritation was mounting, and Karina knew she would not be able to disguise her anger much longer.

Suddenly she felt Derek's reassuring arm around her shoulders, and she heard the firmness in his voice as he said, "Sorry, Mother, we haven't time now to play this game. I want to introduce Karina to Father. Is he in bed or up today?"

The baroness laughed scornfully, her blue eyes as cold as ice. "Really, dear, you should know the answer to that! Your father is in bed as usual!"

"Well, I am taking Karina up to meet him. Good-bye, Mother." With that they left the room, walking hand-in-hand. Once out in the hallway, Derek shook his head in exasperation and said irritably, "I apologize, Karina, for Mother's rudeness. She can be extremely annoying and insensitive at times."

Karina sensed that Derek was doing his best to hide his anger because she knew he was angrier than he cared to admit. She knew Derek had been fully aware of his mother's seemingly innocent but cutting remarks. It was evident in his clipped answers and the tenseness of his body. It had taken all his constraint to avoid an argument with his mother. Karina smiled up at Derek in an effort to ease out of the awkward situation. "Your mother just wants the best for you, Derek," she said, "I would too if I had a son like you." Still she sensed something else was on his mind, so acting on intuition she added, "And please do not worry about me. I am perfectly capable of taking care of myself. You have not known me long enough to see my faults—my stubbornness and temper."

Derek chuckled in disbelief. "Then your faults must be hidden deeply, for I have not seen a hint of one, my sweet Karina."

"They are," Karina agreed without pretense. "I am even-tempered and slow to anger, but when I do, I will not give up until I have won."

"Ah ... that is what I admire, a high-spirited woman with a mind of her own," Derek responded, giving Karina a look that caused her heart to skip a beat. Gently fingering one of her long, golden curls he said, "Karina, I find you completely, wonderfully perfect ... in every way." His gaze met hers and traveled slowly over her body. Abruptly sensing the need to move cautiously and not rush into their growing attraction to each other, Derek shook his head slightly and smiled. "Come," he said, placing his arm around her slender shoulders, "come meet Father."

Baron von Kampler was an exact opposite of his wife, and Karina decided immediately that she liked him. Except for flecks of silver in his thick dark hair, he was a mirror image of Derek. The baron was lying in bed supported by mounds of pillows when Derek rapped lightly on the open door. "Father," he called jovially, "I have someone here whom I would like you to meet ... this is Fraulein Karina Winkler."

"Come in, Derek!" The baron motioned good-naturedly as he smiled at Karina. "Fraulein Karina, you are even lovelier in person! Welcome to Castle Royale! What do you think of our big, drafty castle?"

"It is wonderful, sir," she replied, gazing appreciatively around the richly decorated room. "How proud you must be of this lovely castle!"

Baron von Kampler nodded. "We are, Karina. I hope that Castle Royale will always be occupied by von Kamplers." He motioned to two chairs by the bed and said, "Sit down, please, so we can talk. Derek, have you shown Karina the rest of the castle and introduced her to your mother and Fredericka?"

"Karina has met Mother so far."

"Ah," the baron said, understanding in his eyes, "and she was not in the best of moods, as usual."

"Unfortunately not."

"Well, Karina," the baron continued reassuringly, "you have crossed one hurdle so far; only one more to go."

"What ... what do you mean, sir?" Karina asked, confused. She looked from Derek to the baron for an answer.

Derek came to her rescue. "What Father means is that Fredericka can be rather difficult too at times. She is a very tempestuous and moody person."

"Oh." She thought this over for a moment and then smiled. "Well, at least you have given me warning. If Fredericka is not nice to me at least I will know why."

Derek rose from his chair and said, "Father, I will see you later this evening. I would like very much to get this meeting over with Fredericka, so Karina and I can enjoy our day."

The baron nodded in agreement. "Yes, get it over with, Derek, and hopefully Fredericka will be in an agreeable mood." The baron reached over and grasped Karina's hand and squeezed it reassuringly. "Fraulein Karina, I am so glad to have made your acquaintance. Derek has spoken of nothing but you these past few days, and now I understand why."

Karina curtsied slightly and said, "Thank you, Baron von Kampler. It has been a pleasure to meet you also." She glanced confidently up at Derek as she reached for his hand. "Let us visit Fredericka."

Derek led her down a thickly carpeted hallway and up another flight of stairs. "Fredericka's suite occupies this entire floor," Derek explained as they walked past several bedrooms and a room empty of furniture except for several large armoires.

Karina paused momentarily and peeked in out of curiosity. Apparently this was where Fredericka kept her wardrobe. What fun it would be to look at all the beautiful dresses, she thought dreamily, and possibly even try some on. Her daydreams were cut short for suddenly from a room to their left came a loud crash followed by a shrill female voice screaming hysterically. "Who is that?" Karina whispered to Derek. With a flash of intuition she guessed her identity and added, "Is that Fredericka?" Karina peered around the doorway and saw a tall, dark-haired young woman pacing back and forth in agitation before an elderly woman who appeared to be on the verge of tears.

"How can you have the audacity to call yourself a seamstress?"

Fredericka screamed viciously. She turned and faced the doorway as Derek walked in with Karina.

"Well, well, if it isn't my little brother, Derek," Fredericka sneered derisively, "and who's the girl?"

"Fredericka, I would like you to meet Karina Winkler," Derek said, placing his arm protectively around Karina's shoulders.

Karina looked past Derek into the jade-green eyes of an extremely attractive woman. "Hello, Fredericka." Fredericka was willowy and slender with waist-length black hair, but the allusion of beauty was shattered by her open display of hostility.

Fredericka openly studied Karina for a few moments and then said, "You robbed the cradle this time, Derek."

"I am twenty-one years old," Karina countered quickly, but Fredericka had already turned her attention back to the hapless seamstress.

"You have my dress finished by this evening, and it had better be perfect," Fredericka continued menacingly, "or you will never get my business or anyone else's again!" Tossing her head impetuously in dismissal, she turned and left the room.

"Who would want your business," Karina muttered out loud without thinking. Suddenly remembering where she was and who she was with, she clamped her hand over her mouth and turned to Derek intending to apologize, but he swept her into his arms and kissed her soundly. The elderly seamstress smiled shyly and quietly left the room.

"I could never, ever imagine you acting like her," Derek said, inclining his head toward the direction in which Fredericka had left. "You are so sweet, so pure, so unaffected by wealth and its false power." He lifted her face up to his and kissed her again. "How did I ever find you?"

Karina blushed and stammered in confusion, "It was your hat. Thank your chauffeur, Hans, for running over your top hat." She felt wonderfully alive and gloriously happy. The intense physical attraction she felt for him was still too new to sort out. Should she respond wholeheartedly to her emotions or hold back?

Instinctively she realized that her reserve was weakening, and she breathed a silent prayer for *Gott* to guide her thoughts and actions. She looked into Derek's dark eyes and saw her own love reflected and returned. Impulsively, she reached up and kissed him gently, shyly.

Derek bent to return the kiss when they both heard footsteps in the hall. Smiling ruefully Derek said, "We had better leave. I do not wish to have another encounter with Fredericka. I want you all to myself for the remainder of the day."

The air was cold and crisp and refreshingly invigorating as they left the castle and walked through the snow-encrusted forest surrounding the castle. Karina breathed in the pine-scented air and felt as if a heavy weight had been lifted from her shoulders. She looked at Derek, who appeared to be enjoying the air and freedom as much as she and said, "Your castle is wonderful, Derek. Your family is very proud of it."

"Yes, they are," Derek agreed. "Especially Fredericka; she covets it." He frowned in concern. "Fredericka cannot accept the fact that I will inherit the castle. Even though she is the oldest, the estate must be passed on to the eldest male heir. Only if there is no son would the estate be handed down to a female."

Karina nodded in understanding. "She definitely seems to be a woman who has a mind of her own." And, she thought to herself, one who would stop at nothing to get her way. Karina pulled her hand out of her fur mitt and tucked it into the warmth of Derek's own and continued, "I hope that your father is feeling better soon."

"No," Derek said sadly, shaking his head. "Father is as well as he is ever going to be. He has a bad heart, and his legs are paralyzed."

"Oh, Derek, I am so sorry," Karina whispered. "Your father is so nice. I liked him immediately. How did he become paralyzed?"

"It happened five years ago. Father was making his rounds on the estate, which he did daily until the accident. He would check in on the workers' families and check in at the barn just to make sure that all was taken care of. It was winter, and the roads were icy. Several of the workers had been ill with pneumonia, so Father was checking to see if the doctor should be called. He was riding his favorite stallion, Trojan, when something spooked the horse. Trojan reared up in alarm, slipped on the ice, and fell backward, pinning Father beneath him. The horse broke its neck in the fall and died instantly. Unfortunately, no one discovered my father until hours later. If it were not for my brother, Thaddeus, who found Father and brought him home, he would have died."

"Your brother?" Karina asked in confusion. "I thought you only had one sister."

"I do," Derek said, "Thaddeus is actually my cousin, but we have always been as close as brothers. When he brought my father home that day, he was half-frozen and near death. We sent immediately for the doctor, and he was a long time in examining my father. My father had a broken pelvis, two broken legs, a fractured spine, and the initial shock and exposure had caused a heart attack. The doctor said that if Father survived, he would be paralyzed from the hips down and an invalid for the rest of his life."

"What a horrible thing to happen to such an energetic, vibrant man," Karina said. "Was your father bitter?" She guessed that the baroness would not have been a very caring wife in the face of such devastating news.

Derek stared into space for a long moment before answering. Finally he said slowly, "Yes, I do believe that he was bitter. Actually, he was more depressed than bitter. He had always been such an active, athletic man, and he found it very difficult to adjust to such a sedentary way of life."

"But I am sure that your mother has taken good care of him," Karina replied quickly.

Derek laughed scornfully. "You have much to learn about my

family, Karina. Actually, I think my mother would rather have been a widow than the wife of an invalid."

Karina stared at Derek in disbelief. This was a side of him that she had not yet seen. She had never seen him so cynical or caustic. She shuddered involuntarily.

Mistaking her shivering for being cold, Derek looked at Karina's red cheeks in concern and quickly wrapped his arm around her and drew her close. "We had better go indoors, you are frozen!"

Derek's obvious concern for her made Karina forget her worry, but she was indeed beginning to feel chilled. The temperature was well below zero, and a gusty wind made the snow blow into their faces. "Yes, I am feeling cold," Karina nodded, "is there somewhere close by where we can take shelter?"

Derek nodded as he guided her through the woods. "We have another stable just a few moments from here. It is not fancy, but it is warm and dry, and we can rest there until we warm up." A few moments later they emerged from the woods into a large stable yard around which were clustered four long brick buildings. Derek opened the door to the nearest one and ushered Karina into the warm, dimly lit interior. A horse whickered softly in the box stall to their right and playfully nuzzled Derek's shoulder.

"This is Black Knight, my favorite stallion," Derek said as he fondly rubbed the horse's soft muzzle. Derek motioned to a wooden bench next to Black Knight's stall where they could sit.

Karina sank gratefully onto the seat and leaned her head against the wooden stall. She turned to Derek, her brown eyes clouded with sadness. "Your family reminds me so much of my own, Derek. I was wondering what my mother would do if my father needed looking after. You see, my father has a *geliebte*." She looked at Derek searchingly, unable to disguise the pain and unanswered questions. She said slowly, hesitantly, "Is that how all marriages are?"

"No!" Derek replied emphatically. "Ours would never be like that!" He continued, more to himself than Karina, "The way my mother has treated my father since his accident is inexcusable. Because of that," he continued, "I made a vow to myself that I would never treat another human being the way she has treated my father, especially not the woman I love!"

"I know you wouldn't," Karina agreed softly. She paused and looked up at him, her eyes soft with love. "Derek, may I tell you something?" she asked shyly. "Derek, I … I knew the first time I met you that you were special."

"I felt the same." Derek looked at Karina seriously, his dark eyes reflecting a myriad of emotions. "I want us to be together always, to cherish each other and care for each other." Taking her hands into his own, Derek said slowly, seriously, "Karina, I realize that we have known each other only a few days, but I know that you are the woman I have been searching for. Karina, I love you and cherish you. Will … will you marry me?"

"Yes," she answered without any hesitation. "Oh, yes," she sobbed, tears streaming down her face as she threw her arms around the man she loved. She had not one doubt within her heart. She wanted to share the rest of her life with this wonderful man.

"Yes, you said yes!" Derek shouted excitedly as he pulled Karina to her feet and lifted her into his arms, covering her face and hair with ecstatic kisses.

Karina found herself laughing and crying at the same time. She finally managed to recover enough to say, "We … you … will have to speak to Mama, and she will write Father for his permission. Oh, Derek, I am so gloriously happy! I love you so much!"

"And I love you, my sweet Karina," Derek murmured as he kissed her again. Reluctantly he pulled away and said, "Come, we must leave now and speak to your mother. I cannot wait another moment longer!" They left the stable arm in arm, joyously in love.

Chapter 4

I T WAS LATE AFTERNOON AND snowing heavily by the time Hans guided the sleigh to a halt in front of the Winkler flat. As he promised, Derek spoke to Frau Winkler immediately upon their arrival. Karina found the waiting unbearable as she anxiously paced back and forth outside the closed parlor doors, where she was sure her mother and Derek had been for an eternity. Finally the doors opened, and they emerged, Frau Winkler with tears in her eyes.

"Mama!" Karina cried in alarm at the sight of her mother's moist eyes, "Do we?"

Frau Winkler nodded and drew Karina to her in a quick embrace. Reaching in her apron pocket for a handkerchief, she dabbed at the tears and smiled tremulously.

"*Meine* Karina, *jah*, you have my permission to marry, but … are you sure? Derek is in love with you and will make a wonderful husband, but you have known each other for such a short time!"

"Yes, Mama," Karina replied firmly, "I am sure." Once again she looked at her mother's tear-streaked face and said softly, "Mama, the tears, are they happy or sad?"

"Oh, happy ones, to be sure," Frau Winkler said, smiling reassuringly as her eyes glistened once again. "I am so happy that you have found love. To love and be loved … these are the most important ingredients in a happy marriage." She surveyed the two young people standing before her and nodded briskly. "Derek indicated that he would like to be married as soon as possible, so I must send your father a telegram advising him of your plans. We have much to do!"

Karina smiled happily. Their news had come as a shock to her mother, but Karina knew she liked and approved of Derek and would relay this information to her father. Also, Frau Winkler loved to entertain, and Karina knew she would spare no expense in preparing the wedding feast. Even though they had not yet revealed their wedding plans to the baron and baroness, Karina knew that the baron would approve. But the baroness, well, of that Karina was not so sure.

Karina felt her worst fears confirmed when Derek knocked on the door a few nights later. She took one look at his sagging shoulders and sensed immediately that something was wrong. Derek was standing with his back to the door when she opened it, and Karina gasped in alarm when she saw the worried look on his face. He kissed her quickly and said, "Karina, we must talk."

Recognizing the note of urgency in his voice, she led him into the parlor and closed the doors. "Your mother does not wish us to marry, does she," Karina stated flatly.

"If it were only that, Karina," Derek said dejectedly. "That I could handle because it does not matter what my mother thinks because I love you, and we will be married, and no one is going to prevent that from happening!"

Karina looked uncertainly at her husband-to-be, who at that moment was so vehement in his convictions. Shaking her head in bewilderment she said, "Something must be drastically wrong for you to be so upset. If it has nothing to do with your mother, please, tell me … what is it?"

"This," Derek replied as he pulled a telegram from his coat pocket and threw it on the table. "My orders have been changed. I had three weeks of sick leave left, but now I must report back to active duty in one week."

The words floated in the stillness of the room and settled uneasily in Karina's conscious mind. Only twenty-five words, but suddenly the image she had conjured up of a blissful wedding evaporated before her eyes. Nervously she cleared her throat, not knowing what to say or do. Dejectedly she gazed up at Derek. "Then we must wait until the war is over to be married."

"No! I will not allow that to happen! I have a plan." He turned to Karina with so much love in his dark, intense eyes that she ran to him and buried her head in his shoulder.

"Karina, look at me," he commanded gently, tilting her head upward until she was looking directly into his eyes. "I cannot wait that long to marry you. I want us to be husband and wife before I leave, so we are able to spend our last days together in loving intimacy." He kissed her slowly, solemnly. "I want to hold you, cherish you, love you. I want us to be one."

"Yes, oh yes, I want that too, Derek," Karina whispered, tears of joy illuminating her eyes. Lifting her face to his she said, "Then we must be married as soon as possible."

"Will four days be enough time to prepare?"

Karina nodded. "I would marry you today if I could, but there are so many things to attend to."

"Then we must go to the courthouse at once to post our marriage date and arrange for the civil ceremony. Then we must notify the paper, speak to a priest, and tell our relatives and friends."

"And Mama has already promised that she will have a party after the ceremony," Karina added brightly. She looked away briefly, trying to hide the fear she felt gnawing in her stomach. Even the thought of their upcoming marriage could not dispel the panic she felt whenever she thought of Derek leaving her to go to war.

Derek must have sensed something was bothering her for he said gently, "Is something wrong, Karina?"

Karina met his eyes for a brief moment and then looked away. Finally she looked up again and nodded. "I am so worried about you! You will be leaving me to go back to the fighting and the killing. Oh

Derek, why did this war have to come along and destroy our lives? Please do not go!"

Derek gathered her into his arms and gently kissed her forehead. "I wish that I had an answer for you, Karina, but I do not. What I do know is that wars are started by greed and the fact that the men who got this country into war are not the ones who have to do the fighting. If the government officials who conjure up wars had to fight in trenches and live with the horror and bloodshed, there would be no wars."

Karina nodded bleakly. "So many people think that war is necessary. But all war does is tear families apart, maim innocent people, and destroy property!"

Derek nodded. "People do not think of those things at first … the maiming, the brutality. They are caught up in the romance of war. They see the soldiers, young and handsome in their uniforms and so proud to be defending their country. The soldiers feel invincible, as if nothing can harm them. It is only after the country has been at war awhile that the effects are felt … the brutality, the rationing, the bleakness."

Karina shook her head and shrugged her shoulders in exasperation. "I, for one, do not see anything romantic about war, especially now that my soon-to-be husband is in it! If it were not for this disgusting war, we could be together. I would not have to be worried sick for your safety. It is not fair!"

"No, it's not," Derek agreed quietly, "but then, war never is."

Karina smiled faintly and made a valiant effort to regain her former euphoria. She could only handle one thing at a time, she realized wisely, and now she had her wedding to plan. She went to Derek and wrapped her arms around his neck and kissed him firmly.

"Derek," Karina said, idly tracing the shape of his mouth with her finger, "all that matters is that we love each other and are to be married. We should be the happiest people alive!"

"And I am," Derek said as he responded to her optimism. "Tomorrow we will make our wedding plans. I am Catholic … are you?"

"Yes, we have always attended Mass at the cathedral. Father Mueller, the elderly priest there, I have known since childhood. I would love Father Mueller to marry us."

"Yes, that would be fine. I know Father Mueller also, since we attend Mass at the cathedral whenever we stay at our flat here in Aachen." Derek looked at Karina and smiled impishly. "Now that we have our wedding plans worked out, I would like to discuss with you where we … you … will live."

"Live? I assumed that we would be living at the castle. We will have a wing to ourselves, I thought."

Derek nodded. "We will after the war, but now I do not feel comfortable leaving you alone with my mother and sister. Instead, I thought we would stay in our flat here in Aachen. It is large and comfortable, much more so than the drafty castle, and Nana, our housekeeper, will be there to look after you while I am away. And it is only a few blocks from your job and your parents' flat."

Karina wrapped her arms around Derek's neck in a gesture of thankfulness. "It sounds perfect," she whispered. "Here you are going off to war but worrying about me!"

Derek kissed her gently. "I do not want you to worry about anything, Karina. I will take care of you always." Cupping her chin in his large hand, he lifted her mouth to his in a parting kiss. "I must go," he said reluctantly, glancing at his watch. "Look for me at 10:00 a.m. I will meet you at Braun's Haberdashery."

"I will be waiting," Karina promised solemnly as she escorted him downstairs to the door. "And, Derek, what you said about me living at the castle by myself, you are right, I would feel uncomfortable." She kissed him tenderly. "And you knew."

Derek nodded. "As I said before, I will always take care of you, my sweet. See you tomorrow."

46

"Auf wiedersehen. I love you, Derek." As she closed the door, Karina realized what a caring and sensitive man she was marrying. She had not said a word to him about living at the castle, but somehow he knew how she felt. As she got ready for bed that evening, her heart overflowed with thankfulness for the wonderful man that would soon be her beloved husband.

Derek was waiting when Karina emerged from the haberdashery the following morning, her golden hair glinting in the sunlight. Herr Braun was delighted at the news of her upcoming wedding and had given her the rest of the day off. "What should we do first?" Karina inquired as she admired how handsome Derek looked in his uniform and coat.

"The cathedral is just a short walk from here. We should talk to Father Mueller first before we do anything else."

It took a few moments for their eyes to adjust to the dim lighting inside the church, but then they saw Father Mueller sitting in the first pew of the south section, next to the statue of the Virgin Mary.

"Father Mueller," Karina called cheerfully as they walked up to him, "how have you been?"

The elderly priest arose somewhat stiffly but replied heartily, "Karina and Derek! It is good to see you! What can I do for you?"

"Father Mueller, we would like to be married in three days," Derek explained. "I am being called back to active duty in less than one week, and we want to be married before I leave."

"Ah, yes," Father Mueller nodded his head in understanding. "Many young couples are doing the same thing as you." Pulling a little book out of his pocket, he flipped through the pages until he came to the date they had requested. "Good," he said, writing down their names, "I have you down for the second of January, at 11:00 a.m."

Father Mueller smiled. "What a wonderful way to begin the new year!"

"Thank you, Father," Derek said as he heartily shook the priest's hand. "We will stop by the evening before to go over the final details with you."

"Good." Father Mueller smiled at them and said, "It is an honor to marry you. You both come from good Catholic families. May *Gott* bless you!"

"And you also, Father," Derek and Karina replied in unison. Hand in hand, they left the cathedral.

Their next stop was the courthouse, where they posted their marriage date. This usually had to be posted for six weeks before the wedding, but the rules had been relaxed due to couples wishing to wed before the husband went to war. They then proceeded down the hallway to make an appointment for the civil ceremony to take place. The civil ceremony would be held at the courthouse the day before the church ceremony, and since they would be receiving their marriage certificate on this day, they were reminded that the judge would require two witnesses to sign the document to make it legal. Karina had already asked her brother, Adolph, and sister, Minna, to be the witnesses. Their last stop was at the newspaper office to post a marriage announcement in the paper.

"Can you think of anything else we need to do?" Karina asked as they walked slowly down the street. They walked past a jewelry store with a beautiful display of rings in the window. "Rings!" Karina looked at Derek questioningly.

"I have our rings," Derek said as he smiled happily. "That is, if they meet with your approval."

Karina smiled at him affectionately. "Anything that you do meets with my approval, Derek. May I see them?"

"Not until the wedding, my sweet," Derek said tenderly. "There is a superstition in my family that it is bad luck for the bride-to-be to see the rings before the ceremony. The rings themselves are antiques. They belonged to my great-grandparents."

"Well, I certainly would not want to bring bad luck into our household," Karina said earnestly, "so I will gladly wait until the wedding."

"Good." Derek nodded and smiled mischievously. "You will not be disappointed, my sweet." He took her hand. "Come, let us now go and see our home." Derek's flat was located in a fashionable area of Aachen, built only a few years before the war started. An elderly doorman dressed in dark blue livery opened the door for them as Hans stopped the auto in front of the building.

"Come," Derek said eagerly, guiding Karina up the stairs. "In only three days I will be carrying you over the threshold as my bride." Before he could knock, the door was opened by an elderly gray-haired woman who immediately wrapped her ample arms around both Karina and Derek in a joyous hug.

"*Ach*, Derek, I heard you coming!" Nana cried jovially.

Eagerly returning her affection, Derek kissed her on the cheek and turned to Karina. "Karina, this is Nana, our faithful housekeeper and my former nanny. She has been with our family ever since I can remember."

"Yes, and it is a good thing, too," Nana replied good-naturedly. "Otherwise, who would look after this flat and keep it neat and clean, what with the baron doing so much entertaining. That is," she added and lowered her voice to a barely audible whisper, "until the accident, *Gott* bless him! Now the flat is only used by Derek, who stays here when he has business to attend to in Aachen."

"Nana practically raised Fredericka and me," Derek said affectionately.

"Practically ... hmmmp!" Nana replied with mock severity. "I took better care of you than your own mother, what with her roaming all over Europe for her fancy clothes, furs, and jewelry!" Nana sniffed self-righteously and smiled at Karina. "I have said enough for now, my child. It is a pleasure to meet you, Karina, and do not worry, for I will take good care of you. Derek has asked me to watch over you while he is away at war."

"It was a pleasure to meet you also, Nana," Karina called out as Nana left the room. "I like her," she added to Derek, and to herself she thought that she and Nana already had a few things in common. One was that they both loved Derek, and the other was that neither of them liked the baroness.

Derek was enjoying himself as he showed Karina the flat. It was large and airy with plenty of windows and a balcony outside of every room except for the kitchen. There was a parlor and formal sitting room, a kitchen and dining room, three bedrooms, and separate living quarters off the kitchen for the housekeeper. A white marble fireplace was in the parlor, and another one was in the formal sitting room. Derek looked around in approval and told Karina, "I find the flat to be much more comfortable than the castle. Castles can be very cold and drafty in the wintertime."

"I like it too," Karina said as she gazed around in admiration. "May we start moving my things over here tomorrow? I would like to have all my things put away before the wedding." Impulsively, Karina reached up and shyly kissed Derek on the cheek. "Isn't it going to be wonderful?" Karina sighed happily.

"Yes," Derek agreed, "and it is because you are going to be my wife."

Karina glanced around the flat one last time. "Derek, would you like to come to dinner this evening? Papa is due home today, and he is most anxious to meet you."

"Yes, I would enjoy that. Shall we leave now?"

"Yes, why don't we? We should have a few minutes to spare before dinner, which you can spend getting acquainted with my father."

Hans drove them the few blocks to the Winkler flat, and as they pulled up in front of the building, Karina found herself peering anxiously out the window.

"Oh, I do hope that Papa is home," Karina murmured, "I do so want you to meet him, Derek." They climbed the stairs, and before Karina could knock on the door, it was opened by a tall, distinguished-looking man. "Papa!" Karina cried as she flung herself into his arms.

"Karina, *meine kind*! Ah, let me look at you." Herr Winkler studied Karina at arm's length, a look of undisguised pride on his handsome features. "You look lovely as always and radiantly happy." Herr Winkler turned to Derek and extended his hand. "Derek, it is so good to meet you. You must be the reason why my daughter appears so happy."

Derek smiled broadly as he returned the handshake. "Thank you, sir. And yes, I do take full credit for your daughter's happiness!"

Herr Winkler laughed and put his arm around Derek's shoulder. "It is a pleasure to welcome you to our family. Come, let us eat, and then we will talk."

Dinner was always a lively affair whenever Rolf Winkler was home, and Karina noted with pride how easily Derek adjusted to her family. Her mother adored him, and her younger sisters, Gertrude and Minna, giggled at his every remark while her brother, Adolph, looked up to him as an older brother.

As soon as dinner was over, Herr Winkler said to Karina and Derek, "Come, let us retire to the parlor where we can talk undisturbed." Herr Winkler motioned for them to be seated while he poured them each a glass of after-dinner wine. Pouring one for himself, he sat down across from them. Herr Winkler took a small sip of his wine and nodded appreciatively before setting the glass down on the table next to him. "A good vintage, yes?" he said as he took another sip. He settled himself comfortably in the chair and asked, "Derek, how do your parents, the baron and baroness, feel about this marriage?"

"Sir, my father is as enchanted with Karina as I am," Derek replied, his handsome face glowing with pride. "He knows that we are deeply in love, and he feels that is very important for a marriage to succeed."

"As I do," Herr Winkler agreed. "And your mother, the baroness, what does she think?"

Shrugging his shoulders, Derek said carefully, "Mother is not quite as happy. My mother is very conscious of her social status, and because of this she can be extremely narrow-minded."

Herr Winkler nodded, a small frown creasing his brow. "I appreciate your honesty, Derek," Herr Winkler said as he took another sip of wine. "But what will the baroness think when Karina comes to live under the same roof as she? I do not wish for my daughter to be subjected to prejudice because of her social class. Because of this concern, I do not know if I can give you my permission to marry Karina. It does not sound like an atmosphere in which I would like my daughter to live."

"When we are first married, Herr Winkler," Derek explained, "Karina and I will live at our flat in Aachen. Our housekeeper, Nana, resides there also and will look after Karina while I am away at war." Derek nodded in agreement and said, "I also do not wish for Karina to live by herself at Castle Royale."

"Yes, Papa," Karina interjected quickly, "Derek knew that I would be uncomfortable living by myself at the castle, so he immediately thought of the flat."

"Once the war is over," Derek continued, "we will eventually move to the estate, but I will be there with Karina, and our living quarters will be in a separate wing."

Herr Winkler nodded in approval. "Yes, that arrangement sounds more suitable to me."

"Then, Papa," Karina prompted worriedly, "do we have your permission to marry?" Waiting for his answer made her so nervous that Karina felt everyone in the room could hear her heart thumping madly.

Rolf Winkler looked at his beloved daughter and smiled broadly. "Yes, now that I feel comfortable with the living arrangements, how could I possibly deny my precious daughter the man she loves? Of course you have my permission!"

"Oh, Papa, thank you!" Relief and overwhelming happiness flooded through her body as Karina leaned over and kissed her father gratefully.

"Thank you, sir," Derek grinned, as he shook Rolf Winkler's outstretched hand. "I promise to take good care of your daughter, and I have complete faith in my housekeeper, Nana, to watch over Karina in my absence."

"Derek, you must take care of yourself also," Herr Winkler cautioned. "Karina's mother tells me that you are on leave now recovering from a serious injury. You are an officer?"

"Yes, sir, I am a captain in one of the infantry units."

"Life is not easy at the front," Herr Winkler said, "but you already know that. I was just remembering my own war experiences."

"Yes, I know what to expect," Derek replied grimly.

"After the church ceremony," Karina's father continued, "we will come here for a party, yes? All our friends and relatives have been invited. Derek, please feel free to invite whomever you wish."

"Do you think your family will attend our wedding?" Karina inquired curiously. She looked into Derek's dark eyes and saw a mixture of anger and sadness. Immediately regretting her thoughtless question, she said awkwardly, "I know your father would attend if he could."

"Yes, Father would, but as for my mother and sister," Derek shrugged indifferently, "it does not matter."

Karina guessed otherwise but wisely said nothing. Instead she said, "It will be a wonderful day. I refuse to think otherwise."

"And I feel the same," Derek agreed. Glancing at his watch, Derek said, "I should be going. You and I have much to do in the next few days, and you need your rest."

Karina nodded. "Tomorrow I will begin packing my clothes and getting my room in order. I will only work tomorrow morning, and then I am off until after the wedding."

"Yes," Herr Winkler nodded. "We all have much to do in the short time we have left. Time has a way of passing much too quickly." Herr Winkler rose and shook Derek's hand.

"I like you, Derek," Rolf Winkler said as he studied Derek's handsome features. "I have known your father for years. He is a good man. I will be proud to have you as a son-in-law."

"Thank you, sir." Derek replied gratefully. "It is an honor for me to become a member of your family."

Karina led the way to the door, and as they descended the stairs she turned to Derek.

"Only a couple more days," she whispered unbelievingly, "and we will be husband and wife."

"Yes," Derek agreed and confirmed the fact with a kiss.

"Look, it's snowing!" Karina said as she rubbed steam off the glass of the entry door. "Please tell Hans to drive carefully." Karina turned to Derek and began to button his overcoat. "Tell Hans to take good care of you," she murmured lovingly, "as I will." She looked at Derek with eyes full of love and concern as she thought of him going away to war.

"Karina, you are so lovely," Derek said, his gaze lingering on her beautiful features, "and I love you as I have never loved another."

"Oh, Derek, my feelings for you are the same."

"I will stop over tomorrow afternoon to pick up your things. You will be surprised at how quickly the time will pass. Good-bye, my love."

Karina watched until the auto was out of sight and then went upstairs to begin the arduous task of packing her belongings.

By the time Derek arrived the following afternoon, Karina had her clothing and other possessions boxed and neatly piled in her room. They made several trips back and forth from the Winkler flat to Derek's flat and then spent the remainder of that day rearranging

Derek's flat. The next day was the civil ceremony at the courthouse, and the day after that was the wedding.

Karina's brother and sister met them at the courthouse the following afternoon to witness the civil ceremony. It was performed in a special room, and the stately building lent an air of authority and reality to the situation. Afterward, they walked to a restaurant, where they met Karina's parents for a delicious dinner. After the church ceremony the next day, Karina realized that they would indeed be man and wife. "Tomorrow is the day," Karina said softly as Derek escorted her for the last time back to her parents' flat.

"You have not changed your mind, have you?" Derek inquired anxiously, tilting Karina's face up to his. "You do still want to marry me?"

"Derek," Karina replied solemnly, "I have wanted to marry you since the moment we met. Our marriage is a dream come true!"

"And you, Karina, are the only woman I have ever loved." They paused for a moment in front of Karina's apartment building and clung to each other in a passionate embrace, their need for each other cloaked in the protectiveness of the dark night.

Karina sighed as she watched Hans pull away from the curb, Derek waving good-bye. Tomorrow was their wedding day!

Karina awoke before dawn the next morning with a feeling of excitement that completely erased her drowsiness. Her euphoric state continued as she relaxed in a tub of hot water and contemplated the calendar hanging on the wall. Each day preceding her wedding day had been faithfully crossed off with a red *X*, and the wedding date itself was carefully circled in red. She reached for the ink pen with an unsteady hand and awkwardly uncorked the ink bottle. Grabbing a towel, Karina quickly wrapped it around her dripping body and leaned over to put the final *X* on the calendar. Shivering slightly from anticipation and the cold air on her wet skin, she threw off the towel and sank once again into the blissful warmth of the bath. She took this time of solitude and peace to say her morning prayers.

"Dear *Gott*," she prayed out loud. "As you know, today is my wedding day. Thank you so much for blessing me with such a wonderful man. Please bring us happiness and love and help me be the kind of wife that Derek deserves. Also, please watch over him when he reports back to active duty. Please, please keep my beloved safe, and let this war end soon. In Jesus' name I pray, amen."

"Karina, do you need any help?" Frau Winkler called as she peered around the partially open door. She came in and sat down on the bed and smiled happily at Karina.

"Today, Karina, is the day that every girl dreams of … her wedding day. Are you happy?"

"Blissfully," Karina nodded dreamily, her dark eyes dancing. "I have never been happier than I am at this moment, Mama. Derek is everything that I have ever dreamed of in a man. We are so blessed that *Gott* brought us together."

"Ah yes … ," Frau Winkler nodded, her voice trailing off as she smiled sadly. "I remember how I felt on my wedding day. It is wonderful to be in love." Quickly she looked away before Karina could see the tears in her eyes.

But Karina knew her mother too well and guessed the reason for her sadness. "Oh, Mama," Karina said helplessly, suddenly feeling guilty for her own happiness. "I so wish that there was something I could say or do. I love you and Papa so much!"

"I know, my love," Frau Winkler acknowledged, patting Karina's hand, "but today is your day, and I will not spoil it with my complaining." She arose from the bed. "We both have much to do. I just wanted to stop in and see if you needed anything."

"Thank you, Mama, for everything. I love you so much!"

"If you need me, I will be downstairs."

Karina felt so sad for her mother and wished there were something she could do. Lifting herself out of the bath, she wrapped a towel around herself and began to dress for the big day. With the help of her two sisters, Karina felt transformed as she surveyed herself in the full-length mirror. As her sisters noticed immediately when they stepped into her room, Karina seemed to have a special glow. She had decided not to pile her hair in an upsweep but rather let it loose so that it floated around her face in a golden mass of soft waves. Karina slipped into her white lace wedding gown and held her breath as her sisters fastened the many silk buttons on the back of her gown. She carefully reached for the delicate myrtle wreath that was attached to the veil made by her sister, Minna, and placed it carefully on her head. Finally, Karina slipped her feet into delicate white satin slippers and pulled on her white lace gloves. She was ready. After the church ceremony, Karina would come back to her room and change into her wedding suit. The rich brown velvet of her wedding suit would contrast strikingly with her blonde hair, and the delicate shade of the pink silk blouse would accentuate the pinkness of her cheeks and the dark brown of her eyes. She knew that she looked especially lovely because she was in love.

Suddenly there was a knock at the door, and her youngest sister, Gertrude, poked her head around the door. "Derek is here," she announced importantly.

Karina glanced around her childhood bedroom one final time and murmured a silent prayer. This was it! A sea of faces greeted her as she descended the stairway, but she scarcely noticed, as she had eyes only for Derek.

He was waiting at the base of the stairs, darkly handsome in his dress uniform.

"Are you ready, my beautiful bride?" He bowed gallantly and kissed her proffered hand. "You look lovely!"

"Yes, I am ready, my love," Karina murmured demurely, acutely aware of the handsome man at her side.

They walked outside to the wedding carriage, which was pure white and decorated in gold. A footman dressed in red livery stepped forward to open the door as Karina stepped daintily onto a small bench and into the carriage followed by Derek. The driver gathered the reins of the four magnificent horses, into whose manes white ribbons had been braided, and the horses nickered in anticipation. The driver cracked a streamer-decorated whip over their heads in a signal to be off. They set off for the church amid a crowd of relatives and friends and curious onlookers. Father Mueller was waiting at the cathedral, his friendly face beaming with happiness and pleasure. The ancient cathedral was lovely, as it was still decorated for *Weihnachten* and smelled of fresh pine and incense.

As Karina walked up the aisle with her father on her arm, she had eyes only for Derek. The wedding ceremony itself was short since they had said their vows at the civil ceremony at the courthouse the day before. Now they repeated the words of the wedding vow, and Derek placed the gold wedding band on Karina's finger.

"You may now kiss your bride, Derek," Father Mueller said.

They turned to each other and kissed. Karina pulled away and smiled up at her new husband, tears of joy glistening in her eyes. She felt so thankful to *Gott* for bringing them together, and she made a silent vow to be sure and keep *Gott* in their marriage. They embraced again and walked joyously out to the waiting carriage amidst shouts of joy and well wishes.

Chapter 5

"**A** TOAST TO THE NEW BRIDE and groom!" Rolf Winkler shouted as he lifted his wine glass to the guests. Turning to the happy couple he said, "May *Gott* bless you with health, wealth, happiness and many children!"

Karina saw the smiling faces of her beloved relatives and friends and realized that this was the happiest day of her life. She looked sideways at Derek and glanced again at the circle of gold on her finger to convince herself that this was not a dream. What finally reassured her that she was not dreaming was the delicious aroma of food coming from the dining room. Her parents had spared no expense in the wedding feast, and Karina smiled fondly as she watched her parents mingle with their guests to make sure that everyone was having a good time.

Frau Winkler had been busy baking for several days, and she was well-known for her delicious cakes and pastries. Karina could not wait to try one cake in particular … a chocolate delicacy that had inch-thick buttercream frosting decorated with pink marzipan roses. There were also several apricot and cinnamon *stollen* and trays of *printen* ordered from Lambertz. Lambertz made the best *printen* in Aachen, and Frau Winkler always ordered from them on holidays and special occasions. But before the desserts could be sampled, there were equally tantalizing aromas wafting from pans of roast chicken, sausage, and ham, as well as potato dumplings and mashed potatoes.

Despite her excitement, Karina was not about to let this good food go to waste; she was truly hungry. The citizens of Germany had been rationed to one serving of meat per week since the war started, but it had been weeks since they had seen any meat at all. The shelves were empty in the butcher shop. All meat went to feed the starving troops. Karina knew that her father must have obtained these delicacies on the black market and paid a fortune indeed. She turned to Derek and whispered, "What a wonderful party! Papa has spared no expense!"

Derek nodded as they sat down at the table. "Your father is a very generous man."

"Attention everyone ... attention!" Rolf Winkler shouted above the noise of the crowd. "Please allow me to say grace, and then please help yourselves to the delicious food!" He bowed his head, "*Mein Gott*, thank you for this gift of food. Please watch over Karina and Derek as they start their new life together and bless them always. In Jesus' name I pray, amen!"

The famished guests did not need any urging to eat as they enjoyed foods not available for months. As Karina finished the last bite of chocolate cake, she heard the musicians warming up in the parlor. The furniture had been pushed against the wall and the carpet rolled up so there would be room to dance. The soft strains of a waltz began as Karina and Derek entered the room.

"May I have this dance, my lovely bride?" Derek bowed before Karina as he swept her into his arms.

"Are you enjoying yourself?" Karina whispered as he guided her around the room. He was a very skillful dancer, and Karina found herself enjoying the closeness of their bodies.

"Yes, very much," Derek nodded, his dark eyes gazing into hers, "but I long for us to be alone. This is our wedding night, my love."

Karina dropped her eyes, blushing deeply. "It ... it will be my first time. Will you show me what to do?" She felt suddenly nervous and more than a little scared. She had only a vague idea of what to expect, as her mother had never discussed the details with her.

Derek's arm tightened protectively around her waist as he put his mouth close to her right ear and whispered, "I will show you everything, my love. We have the rest of our lives."

Karina looked into the eyes of her beloved and saw his deep feelings for her clearly reflected. She felt her own love flowing from her, freely given, rejoicing that her love was being absorbed and cherished by her husband. Knowing and realizing this, she whispered, "I love you so much, and I know that whatever happens tonight will be wonderful because you are." Every nerve in her body was at a fever pitch as the physical perfection of her husband inflamed her senses to such an extent that she longed to show him her love. She was ready to discover just how passionate she could be. The thought of venturing into this uncharted territory, a place where she would lose all her inhibitions and give in to her wildest passions almost made her want to take Derek's hand at that very moment and lead him into her upstairs bedroom. She shook her head and almost blushed at the boldness of her thoughts. But suddenly she remembered something her friend and coworker, Maria, had made delicate mention of, and she gazed up at Derek and whispered hesitantly, "Derek, will—will you be gentle with me?"

Crushing Karina to his chest possessively until she could feel the tautness of his muscles, Derek said softly, "Karina, my love, I could never, would never, hurt you. What we will experience together will be so beautiful that there are no words to describe it."

Karina looked up at Derek trustingly and saw his deep love for her reflected in his dark eyes. She decided that whatever mysteries her wedding night held, she felt certain that it would be wonderful because of their love for each other.

Their absorption in each other was interrupted as Karina saw her father wave to her from the edge of the dance floor. Motioning for them to follow him into the hallway he whispered, "There is a woman at the door, Derek, who claims to be your sister."

"Thank you, sir," Derek replied calmly. "I will talk to her."

Fredericka was standing by the front door, impatiently tapping her right foot. She wore a red suit and white silk blouse that contrasted strikingly with her raven-black hair.

"Well, little brother, congratulations," Fredericka said sweetly as they came into the foyer. "I felt it my duty to represent our family at your wedding since Father is obviously unable to attend and Mother is not feeling well. And, after all," she added sardonically, "this is *the* social event of the year, is it not?"

"Thank you for coming, Fredericka," Karina interjected quickly, sensing the hostility between brother and sister. "Would you care for something to eat?"

Glancing disdainfully in the direction of the dining room, Fredericka shook her head. "No, thank you, I have eaten." Looking around the room in mock surprise she added, "I assumed that the door would be answered by your butler or one of the maids. Are they busy in the kitchen?"

Karina shook her head. "No, my mother prefers to do the work herself, and my sisters and I help too."

Fredericka shook her head in wonder. "Imagine that, Derek … you sly fellow! Just think, a wife *and* a servant. You got two women for the price of one!"

Derek's handsome face darkened in anger, but before he could reply Fredericka laughed and tossed her head proudly as she patted his arm.

"*Ach*, do not get angry, my hot-blooded little brother," Fredericka said. "I only meant that Karina is so very fortunate to have such talents, since I could never do such things!"

"No, you couldn't," Derek agreed evenly. "You never did have any talents, did you?" Before Fredericka could respond, Derek gave her a little nudge in the direction of the parlor, where the lovely strains of a waltz could be heard playing. "Perhaps you would like to meet Karina's family. They are with the rest of the guests who are enjoying the dancing in the parlor. Perhaps I might even find an old gentleman who would be willing to dance with you, Fredericka," Derek added casually.

A look of horror crossed Fredericka's beautiful face, and she recoiled in disgust from Derek's suggestion. "*Me* dance with a tottering, slobbering old fool?" she spat out vehemently. "Could you actually see *me*, dear brother, doing something like that?" Pulling on her gloves, Fredericka reached into her purse and pulled out an envelope and threw it on the floor. "This is from Father," she said to Derek, deliberately stepping on the gift. "He insisted that I deliver it to you, which I have done. Now I'll be going. I've done my good deed for the day, and I'm tired of it. Good-bye." Without a backward glance, Fredericka opened the door and slammed it shut behind her.

"Derek, are you okay?" Karina asked cautiously, afraid of the murderous look in his black eyes as he bent over to pick up the soiled envelope. Slowly he wiped it off, and as he did, Karina could see his anger draining away.

"Karina," Derek replied slowly, "when Fredericka said that about you, I wanted to strangle her. Her behavior is unforgivable!"

Karina nodded slightly. "Yes, Fredericka was extremely rude, but you," she said gently, resting her hands on Derek's chest, "you were wonderful!"

Derek looked confused for a moment and then he chuckled. "Oh, you mean when I offered to find an old gentleman for her to dance with! I knew that would make her mad!" But suddenly he drew serious again, unable to forget how his sister had acted toward his lovely wife. "Believe me, Karina," Derek said as he drew Karina close, "I know Fredericka well, and she only came here for one reason, and that was to cause trouble!"

Karina looked up in time to catch a look of hatred in his black eyes, but his gaze softened immediately as their eyes met and held in a silent embrace.

Drawing her to him in a loving embrace, Derek whispered fiercely into her ear, "I will not let anyone or anything spoil our wedding day!"

Karina could feel his tension ease as Derek continued to hold her. She reached up and gently stroked the strong lines of his handsome face, and as she did so, she could see another fire lighting his dark eyes, this time one of passion and wanting instead of anger and hatred. She wanted to leave immediately and go to their flat, where they could be alone so she could give of herself to this wonderful man she had married.

Her thoughts were verbalized when Derek nodded toward the guests and said, "Say *auf wiedersehen* to your parents, my sweet. It is time for us to leave."

"Yes, I will tell them." As she walked to the parlor, she found herself contemplating her new and unfamiliar role of wife and lover. Everything had happened so quickly, and even though she was happier than she had ever been in her life, she was a little uncertain as to how to act in her new life. She looked around at the familiar rooms of the flat and realized that her life would never again be the same. Her father spotted her across the room and knew from her look that they were ready to leave. She went back to her husband's side and grasped his hand, admiring the wedding ring that encircled his finger. Lifting her delicate face to gaze up at her husband, she murmured shyly, "Derek, I cannot believe that we are truly married. Is it really true or just a dream?"

"You had better believe it," Derek responded softly, seductively, as his arm encircled Karina's tiny waist, "because tonight you are coming home with me."

There was such love and tenderness in Derek's voice that Karina felt instantly reassured, and she knew that with Derek at her side she could face any trials or tribulations that came their way.

Her parents were waiting to say good-bye, Frau Winkler dabbing at her eyes with a handkerchief, and Karina's father, embarrassed at this display of emotion, pointedly clearing his throat as he looked at his wife. "Do not believe her tears, Derek," Rolf Winkler said jovially, "because we are very happy to have you as our son-in-law. I know that you will be a good husband to Karina."

Frau Winkler, who was still dabbing at her tears, smiled her approval. "Yes, Derek, I know you will be good to Karina. These are tears of joy, not sorrow."

"I know," Derek said gently, "and I will do my utmost to make my beautiful wife happy."

Turning to her parents, Karina wrapped her arms around each in turn, giving them both a huge kiss. Even though they considered such a display of emotion embarrassing, Karina knew that they were pleased. "Thank you both for such a wonderful party," she said tearfully, "Derek and I will never forget it."

"Yes," Derek added, "and thank you most of all for your daughter. She has made my life complete."

Fighting valiantly to keep his composure, for Rolf Winkler loved his daughter dearly, he cleared his throat and offered his hand to Derek as he said, "If you need anything, either of you, just let us know. This is your home too, you know."

"Thank you, Papa and Mama, I love you both so much!" For a final time, she kissed her parents, and then, linking her arm through Derek's, they left.

"Are you cold, my sweet?" Derek inquired in concern as Karina shivered suddenly. It was bitter cold outside, and the auto had no heat. Quickly Derek threw a robe over their laps.

"Yes, but the … the robe should help," Karina managed to say through chattering teeth. She was cold, but more than that she was scared. Once again, her doubts had raised their ugly heads, and now that she was away from the security of the only home she had ever known, she felt her self-confidence withering away. After all, she had only her parents' marriage as a guide, and their marriage was not a happy one. Turning to Derek in confusion she sobbed, "Derek, please say that you will love me above all other women ... even when I grow old!"

"Karina, what has that got to do with my loving you?" Derek answered, his voice mirroring her confusion. "I love you, and I will always love you. I did not marry you just because you are beautiful—which you are, but I also love you for who you are, and that will never change!" Leaning over, he kissed her tenderly, trying to draw out all her pain and bewilderment, caressing her lips with his until he felt her body relax. They clung to each other, lost in their love for each other, their kisses growing more insistent. Grasping her by the shoulders, Derek said, "Karina, I love you! You are and will always be the only woman I will ever love!"

Sighing with relief, Karina slumped limply against Derek's shoulder. "I love you so very much, Derek," she murmured, "and I am so blessed to have a husband like you." Trying to explain her outburst she said, "It would kill me if I thought you did not love me." She sighed sadly and looked up at Derek, pain nakedly evident in her dark eyes. "I ... I am afraid, Derek. I am afraid that our marriage will end up just like my parents'. Mama loves my father very much even though their marriage was arranged by their families. But I guess that Father never loved Mama deeply enough to want her above all other women. Instead he rejected her love and found it in the arms of a *geliebte*."

Derek tightened his arm protectively around Karina's shoulders and said fiercely, "Karina, I want only you—no other. Our love is special. What we have together is precious and wondrous. It is like a protective shield—surrounding us and protecting us from danger. It will be like that always."

Karina sat perfectly still, listening intently to Derek's every word, her eyes never leaving his face. Her concentration was so intense that she seemed hypnotized. Finally, a spark lit her eyes, and she said slowly, "Yes, I can feel it too. I think I can really feel our love protecting us!" She sensed that Derek had never before confided his feelings so openly with a woman as he had with her. She had always trusted her instincts before, and she would now too because she felt safe, secure, and deeply loved. She would never doubt his love again.

Hans stopped the auto in front of their new home, an imposing three-story brick building where the baron's flat was located. He had generously given the flat to Derek and Karina as a wedding gift. Derek helped Karina out of the auto and up the sidewalk into the foyer of the building. "Welcome to your new home, my love," Derek said tenderly as he kissed Karina and lifted her into his strong arms.

"Derek!" Karina gasped with delight, "surely you do not intend to carry me up two flights of stairs!"

"Oh yes, I do," Derek said as they began the ascent. "That is precisely what I intend to do, my lovely bride!" They reached the flat, and Derek set her down momentarily so he could unlock the door. Once again he lifted her into his arms and carried her over the threshold, setting her down before the fireplace.

Karina looked around quickly. The room was dark and very romantic. The thick, blue velvet curtains had been drawn against the evening's chill, and a warm fire glowed softly in the fireplace. A small table with place settings for two had been arranged in front of the fireplace, and as Karina sank gratefully into one of the chairs, Derek poured wine into their glasses. Lifting his glass to hers he said solemnly, "To the woman I love, who has made me the happiest man alive."

"And to the man I love," Karina replied confidently, "who has made my world complete."

Derek looked at her across the table, his dark eyes smiling as he took her wine glass and set it on the table. "And what does my lovely wife think of married life so far?"

"I love it. *Gott* has blessed us, and I want to spend the rest of my life loving and caring for you." She got up from her chair and settled herself onto Derek's lap.

Ever so gently, Derek began to kiss her, slowly at first, until Karina responded without hesitation. Gathering her into his powerful arms, Derek carried her into the master bedroom, where he placed her gently on the soft bed. Pulling the bed curtains around them, they lay in a protected cocoon of warmth and darkness where no one, or nothing else, existed but their love.

Sometime later, Karina awoke to find herself cuddled protectively in the arms of her husband. "Derek, are you sleeping?" she whispered, as she propped herself up on one elbow and gently traced the strong outline of his handsome face.

"No, my love," he responded softly. "I have spent a good part of the night thanking *Gott* for the beautiful woman lying beside me." Kissing her tenderly, they once again became lost in their love.

Their few days together passed quickly until Karina awoke early one morning with the frightening realization that Derek would be leaving in two more days. Turning onto her side, she studied the sleeping form of her beloved, who looked so young, so handsome, and so dear. Dear Jesus, she prayed silently, please watch over him and let our time apart be brief—please let this war end soon. Tears of fear welled up in her eyes and overflowed onto her cheeks. She wiped them away quickly, glancing over at Derek to make sure that he was still sleeping. She did not want him to know how upset she was, or how worried she was for his safety. She had to be brave for his sake. He would have enough to worry about without worrying about her too.

Derek stretched and yawned sleepily. Turning over, he smiled contentedly. "Awake already?" he inquired drowsily.

"Just barely. What would you like to do today, my love?"

Turning over onto his back, Derek put his hands behind his head and stared at the ceiling. "I must speak with my father today about some estate matters, and then I must stop at the lawyer's office to sign some papers." He paused and looked at Karina. "I have made out a will."

"Derek!" Karina cried in shock. "Whatever did you do that for?" The idea of Derek having a will scared her. It made it sound as if Derek were never coming back to her. She shuddered involuntarily and moved closer to him. "You … you sound as if you are afraid that something is going to happen to you."

"No, Karina, I do not feel like that," Derek reassured soothingly as he gathered her into his strong arms, "but in the event that something did happen to me, I want to make sure that you will be well provided for." Kissing her, he added softly, "You are the most important thing in this world to me, you know."

Tears again welled up in her eyes as Karina sobbed miserably, "Oh, Derek, what am I going to do without you? We are newlyweds; we should be together! If only this awful war would end!" Their time together had passed much too quickly, and now that Derek's departure was imminent, it was taking every ounce of courage she possessed to remain reasonably calm. She saw in Derek's eyes that he felt every bit as miserable as she, but he was doing his manly best to reassure her.

Kissing her lightly on the forehead Derek said, "We had better get up. We have much to do."

After a quick breakfast, they stopped at the lawyer's office. Herr Blum was a large, balding man in his early fifties who treated Derek with a great deal of respect. "Ah yes, Derek, the papers are all ready to be signed," he said as he shuffled some papers on his desk. "My secretary has them right here."

Once the will was signed and witnessed, Derek visibly relaxed. Taking Karina's hand as they left the office, Derek said with satisfaction, "Now I know for sure that you will be well-provided for."

Karina did not look forward to meeting the baroness again, but she knew that it was inevitable. It was snowing heavily by the time they reached the castle, and their trip had taken much longer than expected. A fire was burning in the fireplace in the entrance hall, and they paused briefly to warm their hands as Derek handed their wraps to the butler.

"Ah, Gunter, it is good to see you," Derek said as he shook the butler's hand. "Is Father feeling well today?" Derek inquired.

"*Ach*, not so good, I'm afraid," the elderly butler replied. "The baron has not come out of his room for the past few days, and his appetite is not up to par even though Frau Schultz has been preparing his favorite dishes." "But," he added, smiling broadly, "I believe that your visit, especially with your lovely young bride, will help considerably."

Derek nodded, his dark eyes full of concern, for he loved his father dearly. "Yes, I hope that our visit will lift his spirits." They left and went straight to the baron's room.

Baron von Kampler was seated in a large, overstuffed chair by the window working on the estate books when they entered. He looked up in surprise, a smile of affection crinkling his dark eyes. "Ah, Derek and lovely Karina, come in … come in. It is so good to see you. I have been expecting you." He held out both hands, and Derek and Karina each grasped one.

"It is so good to see you again, Baron," Karina said sincerely. "How are you feeling?"

"Happy, my dear," the baron responded as he looked at the young newlyweds. "I am so pleased that you have married. Now I can die happy knowing that this estate will fall into responsible hands and will one day, I am sure, be overrun with my grandchildren."

"But, Baron, we hope that you will be in charge for a long, long time," Karina responded hastily, alarmed at the thought of his death.

"Yes, Father, you will be here for a long time yet, and you will play with those grandchildren you so long for," Derek said as he glanced mischievously at Karina, "and we will try to fill your request as soon as possible!" Studying his father a moment, he asked, "Do you feel well enough to go over a few estate matters with me? You look rather pale today."

The baron sighed and hesitated a moment before responding. "Well, you know how it is with us invalids; some days are good, some not so good."

Karina could plainly see that today was the latter. The baron looked ill and appeared to be in pain. Her heart went out to him, and she breathed a quick prayer for his health.

"Well, Father, I will not keep you long," Derek promised. "I wish I could postpone our talk, but I am leaving the day after tomorrow, and I must get this taken care of before I leave."

"But of course," the baron agreed, settling himself more comfortably in his overstuffed leather chair as he pulled a blanket more closely around his shoulders. "We might as well tackle it right now."

Seeing the two men so engrossed in financial matters, Karina knew they needed time alone, so she decided to do some exploring. Whispering to Derek that she would return shortly, she quietly slipped out and closed the door.

The stairway they had just ascended was to her left, so Karina decided to go right and see where the long corridor led to. She walked past numerous bedrooms, and when she took another right, she found herself on a landing dominated by a huge stained glass window depicting a battle scene from long ago. Directly to the window's left was an ornately carved wooden door, which stood partly ajar. Curious, Karina peeked inside; pushing the door farther open to let in more light, she realized with delight that she was in a schoolroom. Cautiously she stepped inside and knelt down beside a row of small wooden desks where generations of von Kamplers had learned their ABC's. Maybe she could even find where Derek had sat. She bent closer to one desk and started to trace with her finger the names that were carved into the wood. Smiling, she knew that she would not

71

have been able to resist adding her own if she had gone to school here.

Suddenly Karina sensed that she was not alone. She glanced up in alarm and saw Fredericka standing in the doorway, her arms folded across her chest and a look of pure hatred marring her lovely features.

"What do you think you're doing snooping around like this?" Fredericka demanded sarcastically. "I can't believe it. You're not even in the family one week and already you think you own the place!" She sauntered into the room, her skirts swishing furiously around her as she continued her tirade. "What are you doing in here anyway? Making sure that there will be enough room in here for all the brats that I'm sure you and my dear brother will sire?"

Although alarmed by the vehemence of Fredericka's hatred, Karina felt the heat of her own anger flood through her veins as she responded through clenched teeth, "How dare you talk about Derek that way! He has done nothing to you, and neither have I!" She stood facing Fredericka, her brown eyes flashing and cheeks flushed. "Derek can't help it, nor can I, that you weren't born a male! You're just going to have to accept the fact that Derek is the heir and not you!"

Fredericka looked at her murderously, and she clenched her fists as if ready to strike Karina. Suddenly her expression changed to one of cunning as she muttered, "We'll see about that, my dear, sweet sister-in-law!" Turning on her heels, she leaped onto the landing, slamming the door behind her.

Karina felt herself shaking and drenched in sweat. Suddenly the quaint room had lost its appeal, so she retraced her steps back to the safety of the baron's room. She could not understand why Fredericka had such a hatred for Derek when she had everything that money could buy. Everything, that is, except what she wanted. And that was to be heir to Castle Royale. When she arrived back at the baron's room she found Derek waiting for her.

Derek's handsome face lit up with pleasure as he immediately put his arm around Karina and kissed her. "Unless you have any other exploring that you would like to do," Derek teased, "we can leave. I have already said good-bye to Mother."

"No," Karina replied hastily, breathing a sigh of relief. "I've done enough exploring for one day!" She had already decided not to mention her unpleasant encounter with Fredericka. Derek had enough on his mind already.

Derek shook his father's hand and said, "I hope to see you soon, Father. Hopefully this war will end soon."

The baron nodded. "Yes, hopefully you will soon be coming home for good. This war cannot last much longer. I pray that *Gott* will protect you!" As they turned to leave, the baron called out, "Oh, and Derek, do not worry about Karina while you are away. I will see to it that she is well looked after."

Karina smiled affectionately at the handsome man who had so readily welcomed her into his heart, and she silently blessed him for his thoughtfulness. She knew she had found an ally in this otherwise hostile family.

On the drive home, both Karina and Derek were silent as each contemplated the upcoming departure. All Karina could think about was that they had one more day together. She willed herself not to think beyond that point.

Chapter 6

THE WEATHER ON THE MORNING of Derek's departure was gray and overcast, which mirrored Karina's mood. A foot of fresh snow blanketed the ground with promise of much more in the dark clouds that obliterated the sun. Pulling a woolen shawl tightly around her shoulders, Karina unlatched the kitchen window to check the temperature and was caught off guard by the force of the wind, which defiantly resisted her attempts to refasten the latch. Just as she had the window almost shut, an icy blast wrenched the window from her grasp and smashed it against the building, sending slivers of glass everywhere, some of which became embedded in her right hand. Gasping with pain, Karina looked in shock from the shattered window to her bleeding hand to the snow, which was now blowing in through the open window. A moan of despair escaped from Karina's throat as she collapsed in misery onto the kitchen floor amidst broken glass and puddles of water from the melting snow.

"Karina, what happened … you're bleeding!" Derek cried as he glanced in surprise from the broken window to her injured hand. "I heard a crash and came to investigate." Kneeling at her side, he examined her hand carefully. "Looks like you will need some stitches." Aside from several small cuts, a large, gaping wound extended diagonally from her wrist bone to the base of her knuckles. Grabbing a clean towel, Derek wrapped her hand in it to stop the flow of blood. Gently he helped her off the floor and onto a nearby chair, where she slumped gratefully, her head hanging over the back so that her long blonde hair almost touched the floor. "You stay right here," Derek instructed, caressing her sweaty brow in concern, "I will get Nana; she can sew it up for you. She certainly had enough practice stitching up all my wounds when I was a boy. Karina ... do you feel ill?"

He did not wait for her answer but yelled for Nana to come into the kitchen, as Karina's usually rosy cheeks had turned a pasty white, and she felt herself slipping in and out of consciousness. Stubbornly refusing to succumb to the nausea she felt as she surveyed the blood-soaked towel, Karina looked up at Derek and smiled shakily. "I ... I'm all right," she replied unconvincingly.

Nana ran into the kitchen, bringing with her strips of clean cloth and antiseptic to cleanse the wound. Pulling a needle and a bottle of alcohol from a first aid kit, she set them aside for a moment so she could unwrap the towel from Karina's hand and inspect the wound.

"*Jah*, Derek, you are right," Nana frowned, "this wound will not close. Karina will need some stitches." Turning to her, Nana said, "*Meine kind*, you had better look the other way while I stitch up this nasty cut."

Karina turned away and flinched as she felt the stab of the needle pushing its way through her flesh as another wave of nausea swept through her body. Feeling ready to vomit, she gritted her teeth and forced her mind to ignore the pain. Instead she thought of Derek and wondered how long it would be before she would see him again.

"You can look now, Karina, I am finished," Nana said, nodding with satisfaction as she surveyed her work. Taking the cloth from the table, she wrapped the hand until there were several layers covering the wound. Awkwardly she patted Karina's head. "You did good, *meine kind*," she said approvingly. "You looked as if you were going to faint, but you did not. *Ach*, you are stronger than you look!"

Karina smiled weakly at the compliment, but she felt exhausted from the ordeal. Nana was right; it had taken every ounce of willpower she possessed not to faint, but she knew that if she had passed out, Derek would not have allowed her to accompany him to the train station, and that would have been more than she could bear. As it was, this accident had used up all their remaining time together. She glanced up at Derek apologetically and said, "Oh, Derek, I'm so sorry this had to happen. This accident has wasted our last precious moments together!"

Derek kissed her quickly and engulfed her in an embrace. "It could not be helped, my dearest. You did not do it on purpose."

"I know, but now you have to go ..." Her voice trailed off miserably.

Reluctantly, Derek took one last look around the flat before he turned and said to Nana, "Please take care of yourself and watch over Karina for me until I return." Nana, overcome with emotion, could only gulp and nod her head. Derek wrapped his arms around the elderly woman and kissed her gently on the cheek. Then he turned to Karina and held out his hand.

They walked together through their home, down the stairs, and into a world of swirling snow and ice. The storm had intensified so that Karina saw nothing but whiteness and would have gotten lost had it not been for Derek guiding her to the auto. Somehow Hans got them the few blocks to the train station, where it was almost impossible to discern the shadow of the waiting train. They sat in the cold auto, huddled together under the relative warmth of a lap robe, holding hands and talking quietly. Karina looked at Derek again and again, trying to imprint upon her mind every feature of her beloved—his dark, sensuous eyes, which mirrored his every thought; his beautifully carved mouth; and his masculine profile. Leaning against his strong shoulder, she breathed in his scent of spice cologne and shaving soap. Dear *Gott*, she thought silently, how am I going to exist without this man? Just as she feared she would break down and cry, the train whistle sounded a shrill warning. It was time for Derek to leave. Once again holding hands, they said a prayer together, Karina fervently praying for Derek's safe return.

Cupping her face in his two large hands, Derek kissed her,

gently at first and then with an urgency, as they clung together, each already painfully aware of the ache of separation. "Karina, I want you to stay in the auto," Derek said as he opened the door, "because here I know you are safe." He glanced at Hans, who nodded in understanding. Turning once more to her, Derek placed his arm around her protectively and said in a voice strained with emotion, "Karina, please promise me that you will be careful. Do not go anywhere by yourself. I have instructed Hans to drive you to work. This is wartime, and the streets are not safe for anyone, especially a beautiful young woman like you."

He tilted her head upward so that she could look into his eyes, which at that moment were clouded with concern. "Promise me?"

"Yes, I promise," she agreed solemnly. Barely able to restrain her unshed tears, Karina sobbed, "Derek, my love, you are the one leaving and going into danger, and yet you worry about me!" Caressing his cheek with her uninjured hand, Karina pleaded, "Derek, please, please take care of yourself for me! Without you, I have nothing! You are my whole life, and I love you with my heart and soul! Please be careful, and come back to me!" In her lovely brown eyes were reflected all her pain and fear.

Kissing her one last time, Derek nodded. "I will come back to you, I promise. Remember … I love you!"

Karina watched helplessly as Derek eased his tall frame from the auto and disappeared into the swirling whiteness. Pressing her face against the cold glass, Karina tried to keep him in view as long as possible, imprinting upon her mind how handsome he looked in his uniform. She sat motionless, tears streaming down her face, her body wracked with heart-wrenching sobs. "Please, *Gott*," she prayed quietly, "please keep my Derek safe, and let him come back to me. He has been wounded once already, and I love him so much!" She knew she would be praying this prayer constantly until he returned to her.

"Lady von Kampler, would you like to leave?" Hans sat patiently, awaiting her response. Gazing one last time at the spot she had last seen Derek, Karina sighed dejectedly and turned to the chauffeur. "Yes," she replied forlornly, "take me home."

In the weeks that followed, Karina found herself slowly adjusting to her new life. She had a strict routine she followed daily, which allowed her little free time. Her day started with a short drive to the Elisenbrunnen, where she bathed in the healthy hot spring water that Aachen was famous for since ancient times. Then she went to Mass, where she prayed fervently for Derek's safety. Then Hans dropped her off at her job at the haberdashery, making sure to keep his promise to Derek. After work, Hans dropped her off at the hospital, where she did volunteer work. She arrived home late, ate, and collapsed into bed, where she wrote a letter to Derek before falling asleep. There was little business at the haberdashery, but Karina and the other girls kept busy sewing hospital gowns and bed pads for the wounded. The work occupied her hands but not her thoughts. All she could think of was Derek stationed in France. He wrote frequently, but sometimes it took weeks for her to receive a letter. Even so, he always asked if she was keeping her promise to him by allowing Hans to chauffeur her about the city.

Nana was also determined to keep her promise to Derek. One morning as Karina was preparing to leave for work, Nana came up to her, a worried expression on her kindly face.

"Karina, *meine kind*," she said with concern, "you are going to wear yourself out with working all day and volunteering at the hospital every evening. You have no time left for yourself! Try to do something for yourself also. Visit your family; go see friends. Derek would want you to do that."

"I know, Nana," Karina agreed, "but by doing these things, I feel that I am helping Derek." The hard work kept her occupied during the daytime, but even her fatigue at night could not stop her from having nightmares. All the fears she blocked from her mind during the day came back to haunt her at night.

Nana clucked her tongue in disapproval, her plump face crinkled with anxiety. "Remember that Derek told me to take care of you, dear. How can I do that if you will not take care of yourself?"

"Do not worry about me, Nana," Karina retorted stubbornly. "I know what I am doing."

Slowly the dark winter days gave way to warmer weather. It was March, and a hint of spring was in the air. Karina felt a renewed sense of hope that Derek would be home soon, as the war was going badly for Germany. It did not matter to Karina whether they won the war or not; all she prayed for was the end to come soon so that Derek could come home. It seemed that the end was near that summer of 1918, but the resounding victory the Germans had expected existed now only in the dreams of the most outrageously uninformed. Karina did not accompany Nana to the market any longer, as there was nothing to buy. The only way that food could be obtained was through the black market. The prices were exorbitant, and the quality was poor, but the only other option was starvation. Karina's father knew several contacts in the black market, so with his help, they were able to obtain a tiny piece of meat once a week. Many people were not so fortunate. Karina had heard of girls who were no longer able to menstruate due to malnutrition. She shuddered as Hans drove her to work in the mornings, as beggars were everywhere. They came in all shapes and sizes and were young and old, but the one characteristic they all shared was the absence of hope in their sunken eyes.

Summer gave way to autumn, and still no news of Derek's return. One glorious September day, Karina decided to forgo her volunteer work and take a walk in the sun-dappled woods. After work, she instructed Hans to take her home so she could change into hiking clothes. Dashing up the stairs, she knocked on the door. Nana could usually answer the door quicker than the time it took her to search for her key in her satchel, but today there was no answer. Reaching for her key, she unlocked the door and stepped into the dim room, stopping abruptly in her tracks. With a cry of alarm, she dropped her satchel and ran to Nana, who was sitting on the floor in a crumpled heap, sobbing hysterically.

"Nana, what has happened?" She knelt beside the elderly woman and wrapped her arms around her, somehow hoping to ease her obvious distress.

Raising a tear-stained face to Karina, Nana sobbed brokenly, "*Mein Gott*, Karina, it is a sad day in this household because ... because ..." She was unable to continue as her body convulsed in a fresh wave of sobbing.

"Nana, why is it a sad day? What has happened? Please answer me!" Karina persisted, fear making her voice sharp.

"Because the master is dead!" Nana sobbed, weeping uncontrollably.

"You ... you mean the *baron*?" Karina echoed in disbelief.

"*Jah*, the baron," Nana acknowledged brokenly. "They say that his heart gave out on him."

Karina slowly sank to the floor next to Nana, her eyes blinded by hot tears. Her mind was numb, unable to comprehend such disastrous news. The baron ... dead! He was such a dear, sweet man, and despite his ailments had always looked so handsome and alert. She could not believe the awful news. Suddenly she felt more alone than ever. With Derek gone, the baron had been her only friendly link to an otherwise hostile family. Thoughts of Derek caused her to leap to her feet in a panic.

"Nana, what about Derek? We have to notify Derek!" She hastily threw on a shawl as she prepared to leave.

Nana looked up at her with a blank stare, unable to comprehend what Karina had just said.

"I will be back as soon as I can," Karina shouted over her shoulder before slamming the door. She ran back downstairs to Hans, who was still waiting in the auto to take her on her outing. Karina realized with shock that Hans did not yet know of the baron's death; Nana must have received the news just before Karina arrived home from the haberdashery. As Hans held the door open for her, Karina slowly climbed into the auto and fervently whispered a prayer that she would say the right words to Hans.

"Hans," she said unsteadily, "something awful has happened. I … I do not know how to tell you this …" She buried her face into her hands as she started to weep.

The kindly chauffeur looked at her, his eyebrows raised in surprise. "What has happened, Lady von Kampler?"

Karina gulped and once again prayed for strength. The news would break his heart, and she knew of no easy way to tell him, so she said quietly, "The baron is dead. Nana just told me. She said his heart gave out on him."

"Mein Gott, no! He was like a son to me!" Burying his face in his hands, he wept, his thin shoulders heaving silently.

"I … I know how you feel, Hans," Karina murmured softly, patting his shoulder soothingly. "You knew him all your life while I knew him only a short time, but I loved him too. He was a wonderful man, and one we will never forget. Hans," Karina continued gravely, "we must notify Derek of this terrible news. Derek must be here for the funeral. We must get word to Derek's regiment and inform them of this awful news so they can notify Derek by telegram. This is an emergency!"

The grieving chauffeur nodded in agreement.

Karina wondered how long it would take for a telegram to reach Derek in France, and if they would even be able to find him. After speaking with an officer at the Army office, however, she felt somewhat better, for he assured her that Derek would be notified promptly. From there she instructed Hans to drive her to her parents' flat so that she could tell her mother of the news. Her father was away on a business trip as usual, but Frau Winkler promised that she would notify him of the sad news.

By the time Karina reached her flat that evening, it was late and time for bed. Running up the stairs, she started to unlock the door, but it was opened by Nana. Even though Nana still clutched a handkerchief in her hand, the blank stare of grief was replaced by a look of competence and coherence.

"Have you heard any more news?" Karina inquired wearily as she pulled off her shawl and collapsed into a chair by the fireplace.

"*Jah,*" Nana nodded. "Your presence is requested at Castle Royale. The baroness wishes to speak with you."

Karina sighed, desperately trying to squelch the surge of panic welling up inside of her. A meeting with the baroness was a frightening thought even under such sad circumstances. But suddenly she felt a rush of defiance surge through her body, and she tossed her head, the firelight bathing her golden curls in a glow of red. "I will not let the baroness affect me this way!" she declared angrily to herself. "Derek is my husband, and I will now allow either the baroness or Fredericka to intimidate me!" Turning to Nana, she replied calmly, "In that case, I will have Hans drive me to Castle Royale first thing in the morning."

Hans was waiting outside for her at precisely 8:00 a.m. As they left the city and drove through the forested countryside, which was magnificently colored in the rich hues of autumn, Karina was once again reminded of the wealth of Derek's family. Much of the land through which they were now traveling was part of the von Kampler estate, and, she realized with shock, now that the baron was dead, the estate belonged to Derek. Her husband was the rightful heir, and she had the right to claim the title of baroness. She preferred to be called "Lady," but she realized in a flash of intuition that she was now on equal footing with Derek's mother. When Hans drove into the inner courtyard, it was obvious that Castle Royale was in mourning. Two black wreaths hung above the massive entrance doors, and black cloth was draped throughout the courtyards. Hans stopped the auto in front of the main entrance, and as he got out and opened the door for her, a maid ran outside and curtsied to her quickly, motioning for Karina to follow. She looked at Karina nervously as her eyes darted to a room down the hallway. "Please hurry," she whispered to Karina. "The baroness does not like to be kept waiting."

The massive entrance hall had been transformed into a funeral parlor with the ornately carved wooden casket on display at the far end of the room. The long wooden benches, which had been present when the room was used as a dining hall, had been brought up from storage and set up in rows throughout the room. Karina slowed as they walked past the coffin, but the maid motioned for her to hurry. She led Karina to a small sitting room furnished in red velvet wingback chairs and a matching sofa, where she told Karina to wait.

Much of the confidence Karina had been feeling earlier had evaporated as soon as she entered the castle, but she was determined to ignore her fear so that the baroness would not use that as a weapon against her. She must not let the baroness sense her insecurity. Willing herself to remain calm, Karina lifted her chin defiantly and forced herself to smile when the baroness entered the room.

"Well, it is about time you got here." The baroness sniffed haughtily as she swept into the room. She was dressed in black mourning clothes, but her sapphire-blue eyes were cold and clear.

"I arrived as quickly as I could, Baroness," Karina retorted quickly as she felt her face redden. "I only learned of the baron's death when I returned home after work yesterday, so I immediately went to the Army office to telegram Derek. He should be arriving home in a few days. Also," she continued gently as she felt her own grief returning, "I want to offer you and Fredericka my deepest sympathy. The baron ..."

She stopped in midsentence, completely bewildered by the look of rage and contempt now distorting the baroness's icy features.

"You *fool*! Do you realize how foolish this makes our family appear?" the baroness shrieked furiously. "Did you think that I would forget to notify my own *son* of his father's death? How could you be so stupid! A telegram was dispatched immediately just moments after the baron's death!"

Karina felt her cheeks grow hot with embarrassment, and she looked wildly around the room for an ally, wishing desperately that she had asked her mother to accompany her. For a brief moment she felt as if she were going to burst into tears, but as the baroness raged on, she unknowingly allowed Karina precious time to collect her wits. By the time the baroness finished her tirade, Karina was ready. Leaping to her feet, her brown eyes almost black with rage, she shouted indignantly, "How dare you speak to me in that tone of voice!" She paced back and forth angrily, her voice taut with fury.

"Derek may be your son, but he is *my husband*, and I had every right to notify my husband of his father's death!"

"Well," the baroness shrugged indifferently, seemingly unaffected by Karina's fury, "we will not have the funeral until Derek arrives. After all, the estate now belongs to him."

"Yes, I know." The shock of the baron's death and the arguing had made her feel sick to her stomach, and the only thing on her mind was to leave. Glancing at the baroness, Karina said, "If you will excuse me now, I would like to pay my respects to the baron."

"You may do so when you leave," the baroness replied coldly, "but since you are a commoner, I feel that I must instruct you in the proper funeral etiquette for a nobleman."

Karina watched with disgust as the baroness settled herself onto the sofa and wondered if the baroness thought her so stupid that she would not notice the emphasis she had placed on "proper funeral etiquette."

"You're wasting your time, Mother, if you expect her to digest anything about upper-class manners in such a short time." Fredericka's sneering voice came from behind the partially closed sitting room door. She sauntered into the room, looking exquisitely beautiful in a gown of black satin. "Really, Mother," she continued amiably while glancing disdainfully at Karina, "why bother?"

With effort, Karina managed to check her anger except for an unnaturally bright glitter in her dark eyes. She stood up slowly and faced mother and daughter defiantly. "You're right," Karina agreed easily. "Why bother? I would not learn anything from either of you in such a short time. It would take eons longer than that for you to learn anything worth teaching!" With that, she turned on her heel and marched to the door, closing it firmly behind her. She walked quickly down the hallway without a backward glance. The undisguised hostility of the baroness and Fredericka made Karina feel deeply hurt and achingly sad. She realized that she would never be welcome in Derek's family and never have a close relationship with his mother or sister. Furthermore, she sensed that the baron's death had not had the slightest effect on either the baroness or Fredericka. The baroness was as brittle as ice, unable to give or receive love, and Fredericka was worse. She loved no one but herself.

As Karina hurried through the massive castle, her only thought was to leave, but she desperately wanted to pay her respects to the baron. She turned and walked slowly up to the coffin, her eyes welling up with tears. Except for the silver streaks in the baron's dark hair, it could have been Derek lying there. Hesitantly, she reached out and touched the cold, lifeless body. "Why did you have to die?" she moaned miserably. "Derek loved you dearly, and so did I." The baron had been such a sweet, good man, and she knew for sure that he was in heaven. Somewhere in the castle a door slammed, causing Karina to glance up in alarm. She did not want another confrontation with the baroness, so, glancing one last time into the coffin, she turned and walked dejectedly from the castle. "Take me home, Hans," she instructed as she slid into the auto. "I will not return to Castle Royale until Derek is with me!"

Chapter 7

EREK ARRIVED HOME FIVE DAYS later, and the initial shock of the baron's death was relived as Karina shared her grief with Derek. His grief was fresh and raw, but the thing that haunted her most were his eyes; the pain she saw there made her heart ache. She could think of nothing to ease his pain except to share it with him. She sensed that if she could get him to talk about the baron, it would ease his sorrow and serve as an outlet for his grief.

"Derek," she said softly as she wrapped her arms around him in a loving embrace, "I am so sorry about your father. He was such a special man—so good, so kind. I loved him very much."

"And he loved you, just as I do," Derek said. He leaned his head against the back of his chair and said softly, "I am going to miss him so much."

"I will miss him too," Karina agreed brokenly.

"How did Nana and Hans take the news?"

Karina sighed, vividly recalling that terrible day. "Nana got the news first. I arrived home from the store to find her sitting on the floor in a disheveled heap, sobbing openly. You know how reserved she usually is. At first she was unable to speak of what had happened, and she seemed to be in a state of shock. When she was finally able to tell me, I ran downstairs with thoughts only of contacting you. Then I remembered that Hans did not yet know, so I had to tell him. I tell you, it broke his heart."

"Yes, it probably did. They were totally devoted to him, both Hans and Nana."

"So then I made arrangements for you to be notified."

"And my mother, did she contact you?" Derek asked cautiously.

Karina hesitated, unsure of how much she should reveal to him, but her silence said more than words.

Derek laughed bitterly and held up his hand. "You needn't say anything, Karina. Your silence confirms my fears."

"No, she …"

Derek shook his head. "Do not make excuses for her. I know how she could be when it came to Father."

"She said that you are heir to the estate, and that it now belongs to you."

"*Us,*" Derek corrected firmly, "and when we have children, our son will be heir."

"But first you must come home to me," Karina reminded him gently.

Pulling her close, Derek said, "I want that more than anything, my love." He yawned wearily. "Tomorrow is the funeral." He was silent for a few moments and then said, "I still cannot believe that Father is dead. Even with all his health problems, he always seemed so alive and vibrant. But I know for sure that he is in heaven. He read his Bible every day, and he made sure that we received religious instruction."

Karina nodded sympathetically. "You have had a tremendous shock to your system, and what you need now is rest. Tomorrow will come soon enough."

Derek nodded wearily. "It will be a long and sad day."

Even though they arrived at Castle Royale the next morning just as dawn was breaking, the great hall was already crowded with people. Derek, looking calm and dignified in his uniform, handled the mourners with compassion and expertise. The baron had been much loved, and all the workers on the estate were paying their respects as well as friends and royalty. Through it all, Karina was at his side, offering and receiving condolences. Today the baroness seemed genuinely upset; her eyes were red and puffy as she clung to Derek for support. Despite her misgivings, Karina found herself forgiving the baroness for her past offenses; even if she was hostile toward Karina, it was quite evident that she adored her son. Fredericka also seemed to put aside her usual hatred of Derek and acted quite civil toward him.

Father Mueller arrived and said Mass, and in his eulogy stated that Baron von Kampler would always be remembered for his kindness and compassion, as he had shown his love for the Lord by the way he treated those entrusted to his care. The mourners filed past the coffin one last time before the six pallbearers, all longtime employees of Castle Royale, slowly carried the baron's casket to the hearse which was pulled by two black horses.

Slowly the procession set off down the road the short distance to the family cemetery, its boundaries defined by a tall, black wrought-iron fence. The cemetery was located just beyond a small rise in the road and near a thick stand of pine trees, which protected it from the wind's fury and hid it from view of the castle. The procession passed under an ancient wrought-iron archway and proceeded inside until the hearse came to a halt next to the baron's freshly dug grave. The undertaker motioned for the pallbearers to lift the casket from the hearse and set it in the grave. The mourners huddled together near the grave as they listened solemnly to the priest's words. Karina glanced around at the baron's many relatives and friends and realized that she would not be the only one who would miss him. He had been loved and respected by all who knew him. Karina brought her attention back to the burial and saw Fredericka, who was standing on the opposite side of the casket. Fredericka held a bouquet of flowers in her hands, and as she stepped up to the coffin to pay her last respects, she pulled a single flower from the bouquet and placed it on the casket. Then, kneeling down, she bent her head in prayer.

Since her face was hidden by a black veil, Karina was unable to see Fredericka's face, but her actions of grief were very convincing. Karina felt a wave of guilt flood through her body; she had seriously misjudged Derek's sister. Quietly making her way through the crowd to the other side of the coffin, Karina made her way to Fredericka's side. Her heart was racing madly as she tried to gather the courage to offer condolences to this woman who hated her. Slowly she reached out to Fredericka, intending to put an arm around her shoulders, but a gust of wind blew aside Fredericka's veil, exposing her face for a brief moment. Karina's arm froze in midair, and she recoiled in horror, for the look on Fredericka's face was not one of grief or anguish but rather one of undisguised satisfaction. For the split second it took Fredericka to realize that Karina could see her face, her emotions had been indelibly stamped on every feature.

Thoroughly shaken by what she had just witnessed, Karina jumped to her feet and made her way back through the crowd to the safety of Derek's side. After prayers were said and the service ended, Karina saw that Derek was deep in conversation with a man and woman.

"Ah, there you are, Karina," Derek said, his dark eyes glowing affectionately at the sight of his lovely wife. "I would like to introduce you to my Aunt Elizabeth and Uncle Peter, Thaddeus's parents."

Smiling graciously at the handsome couple, Karina extended a shaky hand in greeting. "I … I am so happy to meet you. Derek always said that you were his favorite aunt and uncle."

"Thank you, dear," Elizabeth said charmingly, her beautiful face reflecting her pleasure. She was the baron's sister and closely resembled him. Glancing up at Peter, a large, muscular man with thick blond hair she said, "We always thought of Derek as a son, didn't we, Peter? Thaddeus and Derek were always together."

Peter laughed amiably, his deep voice echoing off the castle walls. "Those two boys sure could get into trouble, couldn't they?"

Derek smiled at the remembrance of those long-ago days when he and Thaddeus were boys. They were best friends as well as cousins.

"By the way, Uncle Peter," Derek said, "I heard from Thaddeus not too long ago. His dairy farm in America seems to be prospering."

"*Jah*," Peter agreed. "He is building himself a fine dairy business. Someday he will be a wealthy man." Peter paused for a moment and focused his attention on the baroness, who was approaching the group. "Hello, Josephine."

"Hello Peter ... Elizabeth," the baroness responded, extending her thin white hand in greeting. Laying her hand possessively on Derek's arm, she said, "Really, Derek, we must be off. The lawyer is expecting us in the library." She glanced disdainfully at Peter and Elizabeth and added, "You too."

Peter nodded. "We will follow you in a few moments."

The baroness watched as Peter and Elizabeth made their way through the crowd and shook her head. "Ah, poor Elizabeth, such a disappointment to the family, married to that ... that farmer!"

They found the lawyer, Herr Schuler, waiting for them in the library, obviously impatient to begin the proceedings. Glancing at the faces around the table he said, "I have gathered you here for the reading of Baron von Kampler's last will and testament." Pulling several papers from his briefcase, he cleared his throat and began to read. "The full responsibility of baron is passed on to Derek von Kampler II, who is heir to Castle Royale and all its monies, stocks, lands, and securities. Baroness von Kampler and Fredericka are to continue living at the estate, and each will receive a monthly stipend of five hundred marks. Each staff member is to receive a cash amount based upon their years of service with the family. Derek is sole heir and owner of all lands, homes, and apartments in addition to the estate. The baron also instructed that his daughter-in-law, Lady Karina von Kampler, is to receive a monthly stipend of five hundred marks as well as a priceless ruby and diamond necklace and tiara that had belonged to the baron's grandmother. The baron has also stipulated that his sister, Elizabeth, and her husband, Peter, receive a monthly stipend of five hundred marks and that their son, Thaddeus, is to also receive a monthly stipend of five hundred marks. He also stipulated that money is to be given to the church to be used to help the poor." He paused for a moment to review the documents in front of him and then asked, "Are there any questions?"

"Well! the baroness said in disgust. "Giving all his money away to the servants and poor relatives, and all I get is a monthly stipend!" She turned and nodded to Karina. "At least you also got a necklace and tiara out of the deal."

"A stinking monthly allowance," Fredericka said peevishly, echoing her mother's words. "I might actually have to go out and get a job!" She pushed her chair away from the long walnut table in irritation and walked around to the other side, extending her hand to Derek, a hateful look in her green eyes. "Well, congratulations, little brother," she mocked sarcastically, "you got it all—title, land, and money! Are you going to allow your poor, and I do mean poor, older sister to live here in the style to which she is accustomed, or are you going to throw me out into the cruel world and make me fend for myself?"

"This is your home as well as mine, Fredericka, you know that," Derek replied calmly, ignoring her blatant attempt to arouse his anger. Pushing his chair back in dismissal, Derek rose to his feet and said firmly, "You will excuse us now. Karina and I have had a trying day—we all have—so we are going home. Good-bye, Mother," he said, kissing her on the cheek. "I will check in on you before I report back to duty."

Derek's leave was for only one week, and the short time they had together passed quickly. Derek spent much of it at Castle Royale, reviewing estate matters before he had to leave. Karina awoke early on the morning of Derek's departure and stared at the ceiling for a moment until her eyes adjusted to the dim lighting. Turning over to face her husband, she was shocked to see an empty space where he should have been. Instead, a note was lying on his pillow. It read:

My dearest Karina,

Since I had to leave so early, I did not waken you. You were sleeping so peacefully and looked so sweet and dear. I pray with all my heart that this war will end soon so that I may return to you, my beloved, forever.

Your loving husband,

Derek

Karina carefully folded the note in half and pressed it to her cheek, a single tear dampening the paper. Then she placed it carefully in her jewelry box. How like Derek to be thinking of her welfare—he knew how upset she became whenever he had to leave her. How she missed him already! Drawing strength from his words, Karina dreamed of his return. And until that time arrived, she must remain strong and pray for his safety.

As the beautiful fall days grew shorter and progressed into November, defeat was imminent for Germany. It was all Karina heard talk of in the store, but no one knew when the end would finally come. The enormous size of the military had fed off the economy like a parasite and brought the country to near-bankruptcy. The war-weary soldiers were starving and discouraged and eager to come home but afraid of the welcome they would receive when they did. Karina's heart went out to them, and she hoped they all had loved ones waiting for them. She lived for Derek's return, and, to hasten this anticipated reunion, she began planning his homecoming celebration. She was thinking of this one day as she climbed the stairs to their flat. Pulling her key out, she fitted it into the lock and opened the door. No sooner had she set down her things than there was a knock on the door. Karina opened it to find a German officer standing there, his hat in his hands, holding a small, white envelope.

Clearing his throat awkwardly, the officer said, "Are you Baroness von Kampler?"

Karina felt her knees weaken, and with pounding heart she said, "Yes, I am."

"Baroness," the officer continued, "I regret to inform you that your husband, Baron Derek von Kampler, was killed in action on November 6, 1918, near Versailles, France. His body will be sent home within the week. Please accept our deepest sympathy." The German officer bowed and handed Karina the envelope.

Karina shut the door and stared at the envelope, numb with terror.

She could not comprehend what the officer had just told her. *She* was not the baroness, was she? This must be for Derek's mother! But no, Derek's father had passed away in September, two months ago! It was her beloved, her Derek, who had died! Screaming hysterically, she collapsed against the wall, still clutching the telegram in her hand.

At that moment, Nana opened the door, bringing home their weekly meat ration. When she saw Karina, she dropped her things and ran to Karina in concern. "Karina, *meine kind*, what is it? What has happened?" Getting no response, she attempted to read the paper clutched in Karina's hand but could not pry it from her grasp. "Is … is it Derek?" she whispered fearfully, afraid of what she would hear.

Karina nodded mutely and handed her the telegram. A strangled sob escaped from her throat as Nana dropped the paper and crushed Karina to her.

"*Mein Gott*, what are we to do?" Nana moaned in anguish, stroking Karina's long hair. The two women stood there, each unable to draw comfort from the other since they both shared the same grief. Finally, realizing that something was drastically wrong, Nana examined Karina and saw that she was in shock. Her face was ashen and cold to the touch even though she was sweating profusely. Grabbing her by the shoulders, Nana dragged her to the bedroom. "Come," she said urgently, "what you need is rest." Frowning in concern, she made Karina lie down on the bed and then left the room, returning with the first aid kit. Pulling out a bottle of white powder, she measured a small amount into a glass of water and handed it to Karina. "Drink this," she ordered gently, "it will make you sleep."

Mechanically, Karina took the glass and drank the liquid, completely unaware of her actions. Nana sat by the bed until Karina stopped trembling and settled into a deep slumber. Unable to contain her own grief any longer, Nana gazed at the sleeping girl as tears streamed down her face while her shoulders heaved in silent sobs. Derek had been like a son to her, but now he was dead, leaving his beautiful young wife alone and heartbroken.

Derek's body was brought back to Castle Royale, and once again the massive hallway was transformed into a funeral parlor just as it had been two months ago. Karina was present at the funeral but mentally incapable of accepting Derek's death. Shielded from the mourners by her parents and Nana, she was spared the agony of their grief. Still in shock and unable to accept what had happened, Karina felt as if she was floating in a state of limbo for she felt numb. She knew that Derek was dead and that she was at his funeral, but she felt nothing because part of her had died with him. Never again would she be the happy and carefree girl who loved life. Her spirit had been broken, and the hurt was too deep for her to ever be the same again. As she stood by the closed casket, she realized dully that she would never see her husband again, for he had been too horribly mutilated to allow her a final farewell. As the dirt thudded down on the coffin, she knew that the only way she would keep her sanity was to pray for *Gott* to look after her.

Immediately following the burial, the family once again gathered in the library for the reading of the will. "Before we begin," Herr Schuler said brusquely, "I wish to inform you that Germany has surrendered to the enemy. The war is over." The silence in the room was oppressive, so, clearing his throat, Herr Schuler continued, "We are here for the reading of the last will and testament of Baron Derek von Kampler." He shuffled through the papers and began, "The baron's mother and sister will continue to receive their monthly stipend as per earlier stipulations, and may live at Castle Royale as long as they choose. The heir to the estate, lands, monies, securities, and any other assets is the baron's firstborn son." Herr Schuler paused, allowing the full impact of what he had just said to sink into the minds of the occupants in the room. Glancing at Karina he continued, "Baroness Karina von Kampler will manage the estate until the child is of age. If there are for some reason no heirs, the baron stipulates that Baroness Karina von Kampler inherit all his earthly possessions."

"I object!" Fredericka shrieked as she jumped to her feet, her face ashen. Pointing an accusing finger at Karina, she hissed furiously, "How can *she* inherit the estate when I am the eldest and a blood relative!"

"The firstborn son of Baron von Kampler is the heir," the attorney reminded her quietly.

"Oh, come on, let's not play games here!" Fredericka countered brutally. "Derek's dead. *Dead!* And," she glanced triumphantly at Karina, "she'll never bear his child now!"

"Oh yes, I will," Karina replied quietly, turning slowly to face Fredericka.

Fredericka looked at Karina murderously, her face contorted in rage. "What are you talking about? Have you lost your mind? Just what do you mean?"

Karina pushed her chair back and walked slowly over to stand beside Herr Schuler, gripping the edge of the table for support. "As I was telling Herr Schuler just before this meeting began, I am with child."

Chapter 8

"Y OU ARE *WHAT?*" FREDERICKA SAID incredulously, her voice shrill with anger as she stared in disbelief at Karina. An ominous silence descended over the library so that the ticking of the grandfather clock was clearly heard.

"Karina, are you sure?" The baroness stared at Karina in disbelief.

"Yes, I am sure," Karina replied serenely to the astonished occupants of the room. "I am with child, and the baby is due in seven months." Involuntarily she reached down and rubbed her still-flat stomach as if to protect her unborn child from the hostility in the quiet room.

Fredericka shoved her chair back from the table and began pacing back and forth, a look of desperation in her green eyes. Uncharacteristically looking to her mother for support Fredericka cried, "Mother, how much humiliation do I have to put up with?"

The baroness, however, seemed lost in her own world of memories as she smiled softly, a faraway look in her beautiful eyes. "Derek's child," she whispered quietly. "My Derek will live on in his son."

Once again Fredericka said, "Mother, just how much more do I have to put up with?" But her demand was not answered, as the baroness seemed to be in a state of shock and thus unable to respond.

Seething with rage, Fredericka grabbed a book off the shelf and flung it across the room toward Karina, who involuntarily ducked in defense.

Pointing an accusing finger, Fredericka shrieked, "I hate you, Karina! You … you've gone far enough … you've pushed me too far, and now you'll live to regret this … I'll promise you that!" She ran toward the door and flung it open, but turned once again as she was about to leave, an evil smile reinforcing her earlier threat. "Remember Karina," she echoed menacingly, "Beware … for I will get even!" Her bone-chilling laughter echoed in the room as she slammed the door.

"As I said earlier," Herr Schuler continued, clearing his throat authoritatively, "the firstborn son of Baron Derek von Kampler is the heir. Are there any other questions before I conclude this meeting?" Seeing none, he said, "This meeting is now ended. Baroness Karina, will you please remain a few moments longer. There are a few minor details that I must discuss with you." He got up and helped Derek's mother to the door, as she still seemed unable to comprehend the events that were taking place. Calling for a maid, Herr Schuler waited until one arrived to escort the baroness to her room. Then closing the door firmly behind him, he pulled a chair to where Karina sat and took her hands into his own as he looked at her with genuine concern. "Baroness Karina," he said gently, his kindly face creased with worry, "I do not wish to alarm you, but I fear that you are in great danger."

Karina looked at him, puzzled. "What do you mean," she asked, unable to grasp his meaning.

Tapping his fingers thoughtfully on the arm of his chair, Herr Schuler said, "Baroness, I have had the honor of serving the baron for many years, and we became very good friends. He was an honorable and honest man. Your husband, Derek, was also such a man. But unfortunately there are some in this family who are ruled by greed and will stop at nothing to get what they covet."

"Fredericka," Karina whispered faintly, "You are referring to Fredericka, are you not?"

Herr Schuler nodded.

"But do you think she would really try to harm me or Derek's child?"

Herr Schuler nodded grimly. "I do not make these charges lightly, Baroness, but remember how vehemently she acted when she learned of your pregnancy. Fredericka is a vicious, deceitful, and vindictive woman who would not think twice of harming you if it meant her getting what she wants. She has already made it plain to everyone in the family that she hated Derek because he was heir to the estate. And now you, Karina, because of your marriage to Derek, are the heiress. Fredericka is furious because she imagines that you have stolen from her what is rightfully hers. By marrying Derek, you have accomplished what she has spent her entire life trying to attain, which is Castle Royale. My advice to you is to beware."

Karina sat quietly, a bemused expression on her lovely face. In other circumstances she would have shrugged off the attorney's warning, but now she had her unborn child to think about as well as herself. Resting her hands upon her stomach, she thought of the precious gift she carried within and knew that the wise old lawyer was right. She had to be careful. Fredericka was capable of any sort of devious act if it meant her attaining her goal. Finally Karina looked up at the lawyer and nodded her head. "Yes, I do believe that you are correct, Herr Schuler. I would be a fool if I did not heed your warning. I will take precautions." She arose from her chair, and they walked out of the library slowly, neither speaking for fear of being overheard.

Once outside they were able to speak freely, so Herr Schuler paused by the auto as Karina was helped inside by Hans.

"Please, Baroness, be careful," he cautioned once again. "Fredericka will waste no time in seeking revenge. Perhaps you should move in with your parents. There you would be safe."

"No, sir, that I cannot do," Karina insisted, her brown eyes glistening with tears." "The flat is our home, Derek's and mine, given to us by the baron as a wedding gift. I want our son to grow up in the place where we shared our life and our love."

"I understand," Herr Schuler said gently, "but you would be safer with your parents."

"No!"

"Well, I know that you are fortunate to have Hans and Nana to look after you, and your parents will check in also."

"Yes," Karina agreed, glancing gratefully in the direction of the faithful chauffeur, "they will all look after me."

"We will," Hans assured quickly.

Seeing that Karina would be looked after, the attorney said his good-byes and stipulated that she should contact him if need be. Karina relaxed slightly as they left Castle Royale and drove down the long, tree-lined drive. Once again she found herself thinking of what the elderly lawyer had said. She knew that Fredericka hated her, as she had demonstrated this many times, but the thought of her being capable of bodily harm had never occurred to her. Karina herself was not capable of such actions, so it was difficult to envision this trait in another person—especially her sister-in-law. One sure way Karina could find out was to question Hans. The servants always knew what was going on in a household.

"Hans," she began hesitantly, "may I ask you a rather personal question?" Hans momentarily turned from his driving briefly to look at her, his eyebrows raised in question. "What do you think of Fredericka?"

Hans slowed the auto to a crawl so that he could turn once again to study her concerned face. "Baroness, she is hated by the entire staff."

"But do you think she is capable of inflicting bodily harm if she desires something badly enough?"

"*Jah.*" Hans nodded his gray head vigorously in agreement, his chauffeur's hat slipping to one side. "She would stop at nothing to get her way."

99

"Thank you for your honesty, Hans." The chilling reality of what he had just said made her shudder, and she realized just how fortunate she was to have these faithful servants and her family to rely on.

In the days that followed, however, Herr Schuler's warning lost its urgency as Karina found herself battling other problems. She missed Derek desperately, so much that she could not believe he was dead. How could she when his child grew inside her? The wonder of what she carried within her was also beginning to show external proof of her pregnancy as she found her skirts growing tight around the waist, and she knew that the loose-fitting jumpers she had been sewing would soon be the only things she could comfortably wear. Studying her expanding figure in the mirror one morning, she realized just how much this child meant to her. It was her only link to Derek and was physical proof that their love had existed. *Gott* had taken Derek from her but had given her his child to protect, nurture, and cherish. He had given her a reason to live. Without this precious child whose birth she so desperately looked forward to, she would have been unable to bear life without her beloved.

Karina quit her job at the haberdashery because women were expected to stay home when they began to show, but it was for the best. Amidst the confusion of German soldiers returning home to an uncertain welcome, American, British, French, and Belgian occupation troops were assigned to Germany to prevent any uprising. Aachen was now an occupied city, and the streets were not safe. French and Belgian troops were arriving daily, and much to Karina's and Nana's concern, officers from the occupation troops were being assigned living quarters in every flat and home in Aachen. Their household was no exception; they had been assigned a French lieutenant, and Nana was furious.

"*Ach*, the French, they are swine!" Nana muttered to Karina one day after she had finished straightening the lieutenant's room. "You would think he could at least pick up his clothes, but this," she sputtered, nodding at the tray she carried, "requesting breakfast in bed is more than I can stand!"

While the majority of the occupation soldiers were not unfriendly, they let it be known that their purpose was to enforce the curfew and squelch any rebellion that the Germans might be considering. Lieutenant Jacques Pomet, the French lieutenant assigned to their flat, seemed to take his duties as peacekeeper extremely seriously. Karina felt his eyes on her more than once as she made her way through the flat. He seemed to be forever watching and waiting to pounce upon the slightest misdemeanor so that he could report them to the authorities. He even insisted upon eating lunch and dinner with them, so there was little privacy. One evening, Nana had just placed the evening meal on the table when Lieutenant Pomet threw down his fork in disgust.

"*Mon Dieu!*" he shouted furiously while shoving away his plate. "What is this slop you are serving me? It is not fit for pigs!"

Karina looked up in surprise from her bowl of chicken soup, which was mostly broth.

"Lieutenant Pomet," she replied indignantly, "if you do not care for our food, why not dine out at a restaurant instead?"

"I will do just that!" Lieutenant Pomet agreed, angrily shoving his chair backward. "But," he said, shaking a fist menacingly at Nana, "from now on I will tell you what to cook, and if you refuse I will tell my superiors that you tried to poison me!"

"Why didn't we think of that before?" Nana said to Karina after the door slammed shut. "We could poison him and tell Hans to dump his body in the river!" They looked at each other and burst into hysterical laughter at the idea of dignified, elderly Hans doing such a thing.

"Oh, dear," Karina said finally, "Lieutenant Pomet is a very disagreeable man, and I have no idea what we can do about this situation." Karina could not help thinking that they would not have to endure such humiliation if Derek was still alive. But the war had changed everything.

Karina awoke early one morning with a strange feeling in the pit of her stomach. Swinging her legs carefully over the edge of the bed, she grabbed onto the bedpost and slowly pulled herself up, swaying uncertainly in the cold room. Suddenly she felt a violent wave of nausea grip her, which forced her to collapse back onto the bed, gasping for air. Unable to fight the urge any longer, Karina leaned over the edge of the bed and vomited onto the floor, instinctively clutching her stomach in an effort to protect the baby. She remembered nothing further until she awoke to find the doctor standing by her bed, a worried expression on his kindly face.

"Doctor, why are you here?" Karina asked in confusion, momentarily forgetting her nausea.

"Because you became violently ill," Nana replied, gently stroking Karina's perspiring brow. "You vomited all over the floor and scared me half to death. Do you remember?"

"Yes, I remember that happening," Karina replied, gingerly touching her aching head, "But why does my head hurt so much?"

"Because you have food poisoning," Dr. Kimmler replied grimly. "You are a very sick woman."

"Food poisoning!" Karina whispered weakly. "How did I get that? Nana and I eat the same foods, and so does Lieutenant Pomet. Why am I the only one who is sick?"

"Because the spoilage can be a minute amount but enough to make someone ill. And in your condition, Baroness, things can upset your system more readily."

"Yes, you could be right, Dr. Kimmler," Karina murmured dubiously, "but my health has been excellent up until now."

"Your pregnancy is seven and one-half months along now, Baroness," the doctor cautioned. "You must rest in bed for a few days and sleep as much as possible. Both you and the baby need rest."

"Do not worry, doctor, I will look after her," Nana replied. "I will nurse her back to health."

"I will check back tomorrow," Dr. Kimmler said as he prepared to leave, "and remember to eat light so as to not upset your stomach."

Nana nodded in agreement. "Trust me, Doctor, Karina is in good hands."

"I know."

Karina rested in bed for a week and slept most of the time. For the first time since Derek's death, she was able to sleep soundly without being awakened by terrible nightmares. Until her illness, Karina had not realized how fatigued she had become. In fact, she mused one day while staring out the window at a beautiful early-spring morning that maybe her illness had not been food poisoning at all but a direct result of the stress she had endured because of Derek's death. She had tried to deny his death by erasing it from her conscious thoughts, but the overwhelming grief she unknowingly harbored in her subconscious mind had made her violently ill. She missed Derek terribly, and the ache for him never went away. She knew that if she did not have his baby to dream about, she would have gone mad. Even though she prayed constantly, and she knew that Jesus heard her prayers, she felt no relief from her grief.

Still too weak to help herself, Karina spent the hours dozing, reading, and dreaming about her unborn child. One day she had a surprise as her mother came to visit. Even though they were close, mother and daughter had not seen much of each other due to the occupation troops. The Winkler household had been assigned a French general, who kept Karina's mother busy cooking and cleaning for his frequent dinner parties.

"Mama," Karina cried delightedly. "How I've missed you! How did you manage to get away from the general?"

"*Ach,* that man!" Frau Winkler sighed in exasperation. "He thinks I am his personal maid, always ordering me about in my own household! But enough of that," she added, noting with concern the paleness of Karina's complexion. "How is my daughter?"

"I am feeling much better, Mama, but still weak. Dr. Kimmler has ordered me to rest awhile longer."

Frau Winkler nodded vigorously. "You still looked peaked, *meine kind*. The doctor is correct in ordering you to rest. And," she said as she produced a basket she had been carrying, "I made some of your favorite foods to help stimulate your appetite. I made cinnamon *stollen*, vanilla pudding, and purchased some *printen* from Lambertz's. I want to see you in perfect health again before I leave."

"Oh, Mama, thank you!" Karina cried as she peered eagerly inside the basket. "All of my favorite foods and things we haven't had in a long, long time!" She set the basket carefully on the nightstand and snuggled deeper into the pillows. "Did you say something about leaving? Are you going somewhere, Mama?" Karina was surprised because her mother never went anywhere.

Frau Winkler nodded and blushed, and for the first time in a long while, her mother looked happy. She smiled lightheartedly, looking more beautiful than Karina had ever seen her. "It is your father, Karina. He has written me and asked me to join him in Berlin. Minna, Gertrude, and Adolph are to come too. Your father apologized to me for the way he has acted all these years and has asked for my forgiveness. He says that he loves me and does not wish for us to be apart any longer."

"Oh, Mama, I am so happy for you!" Karina threw her arms around her mother and burst into tears. "You don't know how many times I have prayed for this to happen, that you and Papa would be together. You must go as soon as possible!"

Frau Winkler nodded, but Karina saw a look of concern in her lovely eyes. "I want to leave, *meine* Karina, but your child is due soon, and I must be here to help. I will be worried about you!"

Shaking her head vigorously, Karina reached across the comforter and took her mother's hand in her own. "You must go to Papa. He needs you, and as you have always told me, a woman belongs with her husband."

"I know, but I need to be here for you when the baby is born."

"No," Karina replied, "go to Papa. Dr. Kimmler and Nana have been taking excellent care of me. They will not let anything happen. And besides, the baby is not due for a few more weeks. If you delay, the occupation troops could prohibit you from leaving."

"I know," Frau Winkler agreed. "I must leave before they change their minds." She stood up slowly and gazed down at Karina, her motherly eyes still clouded with concern.

"Then it is settled. We will leave tomorrow; the bus only travels to Berlin once a week."

"Oh, Mama, I am so happy for you both," Karina said shyly, "I love you and Papa so much, and this is what I have always prayed for."

"And I too, Karina," replied Frau Winkler. "Our *Gott* is so good. He always answers our prayers."

"Please write as soon as you can, Mama, and give everyone my love."

"I will. Goodbye, my child. I love you."

"I love you too." Feeling drowsy from the excitement, Karina fell asleep with the wonderful feeling that her prayers had been answered.

As the spring days lengthened and grew steadily warmer, Karina grew restless and could not resist the urge to venture outdoors. She had been confined inside ever since her illness, but as she looked out at the budding trees, she felt that she must go for a walk. "Nana," she called, poking her head around the kitchen door where Nana was preparing the noon meal, "I am going for a walk. Will you come with me?"

Looking up from her preparations, Nana replied uncertainly, "Well, I cannot leave you go by yourself, now can I?"

"Perhaps she would rather that I accompany her," said a deep male voice.

Karina visibly jumped and turned to find Lieutenant Pomet standing directly behind her. "You have been standing there this entire time listening to our conversation," Karina accused hotly. "I would not go for a walk with you if you were the last person on earth!" She tried to brush past him, but he caught her arm in a punishing grip and twisted it behind her back, causing her to gasp in pain.

"Do not make me angry," Lieutenant Pomet said menacingly, "or you could be delivering your baby in a jail cell!"

Hot tears of anger and frustration sprung into her eyes, but before she could say anything further, she felt a guiding arm propelling her toward the door.

"We are leaving," Nana said firmly as they walked past a still angry Lieutenant Pomet.

Neither spoke until they were safely out of sight of the flat, and then Nana glanced quickly over her shoulder to make sure that they were not being followed.

"*Ach*, he is a spy!" Nana said in disgust. "Lieutenant Pomet acts like a spy! He watches every move we make! I wonder if all the occupation soldiers are as disagreeable as him?"

Karina grimaced and shook her head. "I refuse to believe that there could be another copy of him in this world, let alone an entire army!"

Nana nodded. "*Jah*, we must not think like that. There are good and bad people all over the world. I need not tell you in which group he belongs." They walked awhile longer until they reached the Elisenbrunnen, the imposing white-columned building where the hot spring baths were located. The hot sulfuric mineral water was known to have healing properties for a variety of ailments, and judging by the number of French and Belgian soldiers they saw coming and going, it had become a popular place with the occupation troops. Afraid that they might see Lieutenant Pomet there, they continued their walk farther into town, window shopping as they went. "Oh, look, Nana," Karina motioned excitedly as she stopped in front of a window display of baby clothes, "let's go inside ... see that beautiful lace-edged blanket?"

They went inside to inquire the price, and as Karina examined the blanket, Nana wandered over to admire an intricately embroidered *steckkissen*. Nana held up the long bag and smiled nostalgically.

"I remember when Derek was born: I was the first to place him in his bag."

Karina eyed the wadding-lined bag doubtfully. "Why would anyone put a baby in this? I would think that it would make him restless being so confined."

Nana smiled wisely and shook her head. "No, only his body and legs are in the bag; he is still able to move his arms. The bones of a newborn are very soft and fragile. It is not safe to lift a baby any other way."

"Well, I guess you know more about this than I do," Karina replied doubtfully.

They made their purchases and left. Karina would have liked to shop more, but by now she felt completely exhausted. Her feet felt as if lead weights were attached, and she had an annoying pain in her lower back. Leaning against a building, she rubbed her aching back, which bore the brunt of her added weight, and realized that she must rest.

"Nana," Karina said tiredly as she set her purchases down, "I think we had better stop somewhere and eat so that I can rest. I cannot walk a step farther."

Nana eyed Karina worriedly, mentally berating herself for not noticing her exhaustion sooner. "You look pale. This is your first outing in a long time, and you are heavy with child. I should have noticed sooner!"

"I love to shop," Karina said, as she attempted to stifle a yawn, "but I just seem to have run out of energy!" She reached down to pick up her bag, but she soon realized that she could not bend over.

Seeing her predicament, Nana reached down and grabbed the bag as they set off to find the nearest café.

As they set off down the brick walkway, Karina looked around at the familiar surroundings and realized with a pang that the nearest café was the Goldener Schwan, where Derek had taken her on their first date. She would have rather gone to another café but knew that she could not go on. Stepping cautiously into the dimly lit interior, Karina realized sadly that this was the first time she had been here since Derek's death. Looking at the cozy, intimate booths with the hand-crocheted tablecloths, Karina remembered the enchantment of their first meal here. It was all so familiar yet so different. Turning to Nana, she said quietly, "This was one of our favorite cafes."

Always embarrassed to reveal her emotions, Nana nodded, awkwardly blinking back sudden tears. The waitress showed them to a booth, and after they had settled themselves, Nana reached across the table and took Karina's small hand into her own gnarled, wrinkled one in a silent gesture of compassion and understanding. "I know," she said gently. "I miss him too."

They made their selections from the menu and attempted small talk, but the day had lost its appeal. As they sat in the dimly lit booth, Karina waited for her weariness to subside, but it did not. Instead, she realized with some alarm that she felt worse. She felt bone-tired and no longer hungry. All she longed to do was to go home. She felt cumbersome and awkward and very much pregnant. Even though her full cloak hid most of her girth, Karina sensed that other women were glaring at her with obvious disapproval, for no well-bred lady in her advanced condition should be seen in public. And she knew that they were also wondering where her husband was. "Nana," she said finally, unable to stand the strain much longer, "would you mind if we skipped our meal? I'm not feeling well."

Nana jumped up immediately, her face wrinkled with concern.

"You might have overdone it today, Karina. Come, we will take the streetcar home."

By the time they climbed the stairs to the flat, Karina's energy was spent. While Nana rummaged in her satchel for the key, Karina leaned against the wall for support. Cautiously opening the door, Nana peered inside, listening intently for a few moments before pushing the door open wide. "Come, Karina," she said gently, "it is safe. Lieutenant Pomet is not here." Picking up their parcels, Nana guided Karina into her room. Going to the armoire, Nana flung open the doors and grabbed a nightgown. She helped Karina undo her clothing and slid the gown over her head. Finally she unhooked the fasteners on Karina's shoes and motioned for Karina to climb into bed.

Karina sank gratefully into the soft featherbed and felt her body go limp as the stresses of the day were forgotten. "Thank you," she murmured drowsily, already half-asleep. The world receded from her conscious mind as she sank deeper into a restful slumber, where she would have stayed had something not jarred her rudely awake. Sitting up in bed and confused as to what had awakened her, she was about to sink back into bed when she felt vaguely uncomfortable and realized that the lower half of her nightgown was wet. Frantically she reached under the bed with her foot, groping for the chamber pot, acutely embarrassed but bewildered at her apparent accident. She was halfway out of bed when a cramping pain seized her abdomen, causing her to cry out in pain. It was like the cramping she experienced during her menses but a hundredfold more severe. Confused, Karina reached into the recesses of her mind, desperately trying to recall the few bits of information she had been told about childbirth. As the cramping began again, Karina realized that she must be going into labor and that she had awakened with a soaking-wet gown because her water sac had broken. Struggling to her feet, Karina slipped off her wet nightclothes and wrapped a wool robe around her shivering, naked body. "Nana," she cried loudly, making her way slowly out of her room into the long hall. Nana's room was at the very end. She made her way slowly, groping blindly along the wall with one hand while supporting her bulging abdomen with her left arm. Halfway to Nana's room, Karina slumped against the wall and moaned painfully as another wave of cramps engulfed her tortured body. The cramping was more severe now and lasting longer. "Nana," she screamed in anguish, "please hear me … I'm in labor! She stood, helpless to move until the contraction subsided.

The door to Nana's room opened, and Nana stumbled out, rubbing her sleepy eyes in confusion. Seeing Karina slumped against the wall, she ran to her side and guided her slowly back to her room. "Just a little ways more, Karina," Nana coaxed gently, "and you will be back in your bed."

They reached the room just as another contraction started, and Karina sank onto the bed, doubled over in pain. When it ended, she lay back on the pillow, her face contorted in fear.

"Nana, am I in labor?"

Nana nodded and smiled convincingly. *"Jah,* but you are doing just fine. Just try to relax between contractions; do not fight them. You will need all your strength for the delivery."

Her soothing voice and reassuring manner helped Karina relax and realize that the pain she was enduring was a normal part of childbirth. She lay back on the pillow, her golden blonde hair loose about her face and her dark eyes enormous with a mixture of wonder and fear. Just as she felt herself start to drift off to sleep, another contraction started, and she braced herself as it rose to a crescendo and slowly dissipated. "Nana," she asked after the contraction had relaxed its grip, "how long will these contractions last?"

Nana glanced at the clock on the nightstand. "Not too much longer; your time is very near now. I must leave to get the doctor."

Karina gasped and grabbed Nana's hand. "But I will be here by myself! What if something happens?"

Smoothing the damp hair from Karina's sweating brow, Nana said soothingly, "Nothing is going to happen except that your contractions will come more often and last longer, but that is what is supposed to happen. I will be back with Dr. Kimmler before anything else occurs."

Karina watched helplessly as Nana fastened her cloak. She thought that Nana started to speak to her, but she did not hear what it was for she was in the grips of another contraction. She suffered through one after another in rapid succession until she lay panting from the exertion. Wearily, she wiped her perspiring brow and closed her eyes. "Oh, Derek," she whimpered in anguish, "our son is about to be born. How I wish you were here to see him!" Covering her eyes with her hands, she wept bitterly. Suddenly she felt a cold, soothing hand caress her damp forehead, and she felt her body sag with relief. "Nana, thank goodness, you're back. What are *you* doing here?" She recoiled in horror, for she found herself staring into the face of Lieutenant Jacques Pomet. Grabbing the blanket, she pulled it up around her sweating naked shoulders, feeling hideously embarrassed that a man other than her husband should witness her in this condition. Struggling to sit up, she demanded, "Get out of my room, you … you swine, or …" Her threat was cut short as she gasped in agony and clutched her stomach as another contraction engulfed her body. Through the pain, she dimly heard Lieutenant Pomet mumbling something, but she did not understand him until the contraction had subsided.

"Ah, *cherie*," he said comfortingly, "I cannot help you with the pain, but I can make you more comfortable. Here, take a sip of water."

Karina felt strong, masculine hands gently lift her head as a cool glass touched her parched lips. Opening her pain-glazed eyes, she saw Lieutenant Pomet and instinctively recoiled in disgust. But once again gentle hands held her head as a glass touched her lips. She looked again and saw Derek. Her mind reeled in confusion; she must be hallucinating from the pain. Derek was dead! But when she looked again she saw her beloved, offering her water to comfort her. She took a sip. It felt wonderfully cool on her dry, parched throat. She smiled up at her husband and said tenderly, "Derek, oh, Derek, I love you so much!" She lay back on the pillow, smiling contentedly. Suddenly she felt another contraction building, but strangely it did not seem to hurt nearly as much as it had before. In fact, Karina realized drowsily as she felt the tension leaving her exhausted body, she felt as if she could finally fall asleep.

"Doctor, what has happened to her?" Nana cried in concern, throwing her cape on the floor. "I was not gone more than one half hour." Panic-stricken, she tried to rouse the still figure in the bed. "She looks as if she has fainted!"

"She does indeed," Dr. Kimmler replied. "We have to rouse her somehow. Otherwise, the baby will die!"

Karina felt blissfully groggy until she felt someone rudely shaking her and shouting in her ear. Shrugging in anger, she attempted to turn over but found herself sitting up seconds later gasping for air as cold water hit her in the face. "Why did you do that?" she sputtered in anger, desperately trying to ignore the overwhelming fatigue that had gripped her.

"Baroness, listen to me!" Dr. Kimmler shouted gruffly, literally prying her eyes open. "You have got to stay awake, you hear me? You have got to help me deliver this baby! Push as hard as you can, otherwise your baby will die!"

Frightened by his roughness, Karina gritted her teeth and pushed with all her strength and then again and again while Dr. Kimmler shouted encouragement.

"Push again, once more … I can see the head!"

Karina fought the numbing drowsiness and pushed with every ounce of strength she possessed until she heard a faint cry. Holding up a tiny body for her to see, Dr. Kimmler turned the infant upside down and slapped its bottom. Karina waited fearfully as nothing happened, but then the infant wailed lustily, and Karina sighed with relief.

Wiping tears of joy from her eyes, Nana pronounced, "Ach, a wonderful, healthy boy! Thanks be to *Gott!*" They both watched as Dr. Kimmler handed the tiny bundle to Karina for her inspection.

"What are you going to name your new son, Baroness?" Dr. Kimmler asked, smiling down at mother and child.

Karina looked at her precious son and said without hesitation, "Derek."

Nodding approvingly, Nana confided, "He looks just like Derek; he is the image of his father."

Karina snuggled the baby close so that he could nurse, and she felt that some of her pain had eased. Gently tracing her finger over her son's tiny face, she marveled at the perfection of every feature. She could have admired him forever, but she felt her body succumbing to another wave of exhaustion. She handed the baby to Nana and fell asleep.

"*Ach,*" Nana nodded in understanding. "Karina is such a tiny thing, and her first child too; the birth completely wore her out."

Dr. Kimmler did not answer immediately, for he was deep in thought. Finally he said, his brow puckered in puzzlement, "In all my years of delivering babies, I have yet to see a woman too exhausted to deliver her child! He looked around the room suspiciously. "Something happened here before you and I arrived. Someone did something to the baroness, I am sure of it!" Putting on his coat and hat, Dr. Kimmler said, "Send for me the minute the baroness awakens. I want to talk to her!"

Chapter 9

"I NEVER REALIZED HOW OFTEN BABIES eat!" Karina exclaimed as Nana handed her wailing son to her to be nursed.

Nana agreed. "The milk does not stay with them very long. I tried to hold off as long as possible so that you could sleep, but," she nodded to the baby, "your son was starving!"

Karina yawned sleepily and could have easily fallen back asleep were it not for her hungry son. Barely able to keep her eyes open, she yawned again and asked, "Why am I so tired?"

"Childbirth is a strenuous experience. It is not something you recover from overnight, but Dr. Kimmler said he had never seen anyone too sleepy to deliver their baby! You were asleep when we arrived and could not be roused. Dr. Kimmler had to throw cold water on your face to rouse you!"

Karina nodded, perplexed. "I cannot understand why I was so fatigued. I was alert when you left to get Dr. Kimmler, and then Derek gave me a drink of water. I was in so much pain." Her voice trailed off as she realized what she had said. Her eyes filled with tears. "I said that Derek gave me a drink of water, didn't I? How could he? He is dead!"

She paused. "What I meant to say is that Lieutenant Pomet gave me a drink of water."

"Lieutenant Pomet was here? He gave you a drink of water?" Nana asked sharply.

Karina shivered, involuntarily pulling the blankets up around her shoulders. "I started to shout at him because I was so embarrassed, but then another contraction started. I was in so much pain that when I looked up again, I thought it was Derek standing there. And he gave me a drink of water."

"That French swine!" Nana said, "I knew he could not be trusted! Always poking his nose in our business, threatening to turn us in to the authorities! He had something to do with your fatigue, I am sure of it!"

Dr. Kimmler confirmed Nana's suspicions after Karina related the story to him.

"You think I was drugged?" Karina asked, astonished.

Dr. Kimmler nodded seriously, his mouth set in a grim line. "I think that Lieutenant Pomet tried to kill you. If you had drunk the entire contents of that glass of water, it would have killed you and the baby. We probably surprised him when we returned. He did not have time to give you the rest of the water."

"And I did not even check to see if Lieutenant Pomet was in his room when I returned with Dr. Kimmler," Nana said, "because we were so worried about you, Karina."

Silence settled over the room. Karina was the first to speak. "I do not know why I should be so surprised at all this," she said. "I have been told once already that my life is in danger."

"By whom?"

"The lawyer. At the reading of Derek's will." Karina turned to Nana. "Remember when Herr Schuler requested that everyone but me leave the room? It was then that he voiced his suspicions regarding Fredericka. How she despised me because of my inheritance, and how she could not be trusted. He was convinced that she would try anything to get her way."

"And he was right," Nana said. "Fredericka is a vicious, vindictive woman. She would definitely hate you for inheriting what she considers to be hers. But what of Lieutenant Pomet? Why did he try to harm you?"

Karina shrugged helplessly. "Perhaps because of the war, and he is taking it out on me in particular because he is living with us."

"Whatever the reason," Dr. Kimmler cautioned, "you must keep an eye on Lieutenant Pomet. Do not trust him under any circumstances."

But in the weeks following little Derek's birth, Dr. Kimmler's words of warning grew dim as Karina immersed herself in the joys of motherhood. Never before had she seen such an intelligent or happy baby! Nana was just as attached to little Derek as she, always willing to hold him or rock him to sleep. The baby filled a void in their lives and gave them a reason to live. But even the love she felt for her child could not stop the ache Karina felt whenever she thought of her husband and how proud he would have been of their son.

"Your son is hungry again," Nana said, handing the baby to Karina. "Did I startle you?"

Karina looked up guiltily. "I am sorry, Nana," she apologized, wiping away her tears. "I was dreaming of Derek, and I did not hear you."

Nana sat down next to Karina. Frowning slightly, she studied Karina for several moments before speaking. "You have to remarry, *meine* Karina," she said gently. "You have to tuck away the memories of Derek in your heart and close the door on them." Wiping away tears of her own, Nana patted Karina's arm in understanding. "I know how you feel. I loved Derek also. He was like a son to me. But it breaks my heart to see you mourning so. You are so young and beautiful but wearing widow's clothes! And with a new baby too! Oh, Karina, how I wish I could help—oh, how I wish I could!" She buried her face in her hands, her shoulders shaking with sobs.

Karina knew she would have lost all control of her emotions if it were not for the fact that she suddenly found herself consoling Nana instead of the opposite. She had grown to love the faithful housekeeper, and her heart went out to her, for Karina knew she was not the only one who missed Derek. Nana had told her more

116

than once that Derek had been like a son to her, so Karina knew she was telling her to remarry because she cared about Karina and little Derek. "Oh, Nana," Karina said sadly, "the only man I can think of is Derek. Even though we were only married a short while and separated by war, I have enough wonderful memories to last me a lifetime, and," she whispered looking at her son, "more than enough to share with little Derek."

"*Nein*, Karina," Nana disagreed as she dried her tears, "memories fade. You must make a new life for you and your son. He needs a father."

"You and I can take care of little Derek just fine," Karina replied stubbornly. "We will love him and groom him to run the estate when the time comes. We can do it!"

Still Nana disagreed. "You are forgetting one thing, Karina, and that is that I am an old woman. I will not live forever; my remaining days are dwindling quickly. And then you would be alone in that massive castle … with the baroness and Fredericka."

"I know, Nana," Karina agreed, her voice taunt with desperation, "but what are my choices? I know that if I expect little Derek to run the estate someday, we will eventually have to live there. Without you or Hans, I would have no friends in that foreboding household. But at least little Derek would have a grandmother … a blood relative who would hopefully love him. But if I were to remarry, how could I ever be sure whether the man was marrying me because of love or because of my wealth? Housing is scarce; no buildings have been constructed since the war began, so most newlyweds have to move in with their parents. But if a man were to marry a widow, look at all the advantages! She has a house, furnishings, and money in the bank, which would otherwise take years of scrimping and saving to acquire! But the most important consideration," Karina continued, her dark eyes swimming with unshed tears, "is how could I be sure that another man would love my son as his own? If he did not, that I could not bear!"

Nana rocked back and forth silently, her crinkled face solemn. "I wish I had an answer for you, Karina. I am just so worried for your safety."

Karina looked up and glanced in the direction of Lieutenant Pomet's room. "If he did try to kill me once, then he will most likely try again."

One sunny, crisp fall day after Karina, little Derek, and Nana had just returned to the flat from a walk, there was a knock on the door. Karina opened it to find the postman standing there holding a letter. Her first thought was that it was from her mother, since she wrote frequently, always eager for news about little Derek, but Karina was wrong.

Tipping his hat respectfully, the postman handed the letter to Karina. "This came a long ways, Baroness. It comes from America."

"Thank you so much," Karina said as she looked curiously at the unfamiliar handwriting on the envelope. As she tore it open, a paper fell out and fluttered to the floor. Karina picked it up and saw that it was the picture of a young man. The letter was written on thick, expensive bond paper in bold, expansive handwriting. Seating herself in the wingback chair before the fireplace she read:

Meine dearest Baroness von Kampler:

Please allow me to introduce myself. My name is Thaddeus Conterweitis, first cousin of your late husband, Derek von Kampler. Please accept my heartfelt sympathy and grief; Derek and I were very close. I will miss him immensely, as I know you do too. As you probably know, Derek and I were like brothers, so I feel the shock of his death as deeply as if someone had plunged a knife through my heart. Derek and I corresponded regularly, and through his letters I feel that I know you. In fact, I am looking at your photo as I pen this letter; it is a picture of you and Derek taken on your wedding day. You made Derek so happy, Baroness Karina. His letters were always about you. He never ceased to marvel at your beauty, charm, and goodness. Through Derek I have come to know and admire you. I also feel that we have much in common since we both loved Derek. Because of this love we share, I feel a sense of protectiveness toward you. What I am trying to say, Baroness Karina, is that through Derek, I have fallen in love with you, and I feel that Derek would have wanted me to look after you.

I realize right now that you are sick with grief and most likely will think this confession of my admiration and love for you to be in the poorest of taste. But, Karina, please remember that I am speaking from the depths of my heart—the same heart that also loved Derek—and before you close your mind on this entire matter, allow me to tell you something about myself. I come from a family of eight children; I am the youngest son. My mother and Derek's father were brother and sister. My father owns a large dairy farm, and we were prosperous even though my lineage does not include a title such as Derek's. My parents insisted that all of us children attend school, but my first love was and still is dairy farming. I always dreamed of owning my own farm, but since I was the youngest son, I knew that I would never inherit my father's farm. Being an ambitious man, I vowed to save my money and purchase a farm of my own. Then came talk of war, and suddenly I found myself confronting a huge problem. I would not be able to start a farm if Germany went to war because I would have to serve in the military. It looked as if I would have to wait until after the war to pursue my dream. But then I recalled a conversation I had with a friend some months earlier about America. My friend's brother had moved to America and sent letters home urging my friend to join him. I too had read information about America—of the endless stretches of fertile land just waiting to be farmed, and of the unlimited opportunities that existed for anyone hardworking and ambitious enough to pursue them. I thought about it and made up my mind: I would emigrate to America and become a wealthy man.

I have been here over six years now, and my dairy business is prospering. As much as I love this country, however, I am lonely. I have made many new friends here, but I long for a wife to share my life with. I have made the acquaintance of many American women, and although they are attractive and charming, I realize that it is a German girl I wish to make my wife.

Karina, will you marry me? Will you do me the honor of coming to America to be my wife? I realize that you know very little about me, but I love you, and I know in time that you will learn to love me too. I am kindhearted and generous and have no character flaws as far as I can ascertain. I will be a tender and loving husband, and you will lack nothing in physical comforts. If you decide to accept my proposal, you will travel in first-class luxury from

Germany to New York. I will await you, and from there we will travel by train to Columbus, Wisconsin. My farm is located five miles south of there.

Please, please come to me, Karina. I am very worried about your safety. Your well-being is of the utmost importance to me. The war was a terrible ordeal to endure, and postwar Germany is not a safe place for a young widow. Please think of what Derek would want you to do; he would not want you to be alone. Baroness Karina, I will love you as Derek did. Please come to me."

Most affectionately yours,

Herr Thaddeus Conterweitis

"Please think of what Derek would want you to do. I will love you as Derek did." Karina sat motionless as she reread the lines over and over again. Finally, she noticed the paper that had fallen out of the envelope. It was a photo of Thaddeus. He was dressed in a stylish, dark, three-piece suit. He was standing next to a wingback chair, his left hand resting casually on the back, and he appeared to be very tall and ruggedly handsome. His thick, wavy hair was very fair and parted on the left, curling partially over his high forehead. He had a meticulously groomed handlebar moustache, which complemented his straight teeth and square chin. Karina especially liked his eyes; his gaze was direct, friendly, and honest. Although she did not remember much about him, she did remember Derek speaking of Thaddeus often and with the highest regard, and she did remember meeting his parents at both funerals.

Fingering the letter thoughtfully, she got up and went into the kitchen, where Nana was preparing dinner. Looking up from her work, Nana asked, "Who was that at the door before?"

"It was the postman with a letter from America." Holding it out to Nana she said, "Sit down and read this."

Wiping her hands on her apron, Nana carefully unfolded the papers and read in silence. Finally she looked up, a look of happiness creasing her face. "Karina, *meine kind*, this is your answer! You must go to America and marry Thaddeus! He will make you a wonderful husband and love little Derek as his own!"

Karina shook her head slowly, a look of bewilderment on her lovely face. "I do not know what to do, Nana! I do not really know anything about Thaddeus, and America is so far away!"

Patting her arm reassuringly, Nana said, "I know Thaddeus well. He and Derek were inseparable from the time they were toddlers. Thad ... *ach* ... he is a big bear of a man, but his heart ... it is as soft as freshly churned butter. I can remember him as a child—he was always tending to some sick or injured animal. He could not bear to see any creature in pain. His feelings run deep." Nana nodded in satisfaction as if the matter were already settled. Nana inquired, "When will you leave?"

"Are you so eager to be rid of us?" Karina teased and then grew serious. Her dark eyes held a faraway look as she looked at Nana searchingly. "I do not know if I could ever leave my homeland and family, and little Derek belongs here. After all, he is heir to the estate."

"Oh, Karina, that is years away!" Nana said in exasperation. "What you need now is a safe environment for you and your son to heal and prosper. And postwar Germany is no such place!"

Karina stared unseeing at Nana, agreeing with all that Nana had said yet still unconvinced. "Things are not so bad, Nana, really they aren't," she said with a half-hearted smile.

Nana shook her head in disagreement and shook a finger at Karina in mock anger. "You might be able to fool yourself, Karina, but me, you cannot fool," Nana muttered as she returned to her work.

Karina thought of Nana's words more than once a few nights later as she wrung out a washcloth in a basin of cool water and placed it on little Derek's feverish forehead. She looked at his flushed cheeks in alarm and guessed that his temperature must be at least 40 degrees

Celsius. "Nana, do you think I should go for the doctor?" she asked anxiously when Derek threw up again.

Nana looked in concern at the restless, feverish baby and nodded gravely. "We have a very sick child here, Karina. Go get Dr. Kimmler at once ... and hurry!"

The urgency in Nana's voice made her even more frightened than she already was as she hurriedly grabbed her cloak and raced down the stairs into the dark, cold night. As she ran along the deserted cobblestone street, she prayed that she would not get caught. It was well past curfew and if apprehended, she would be thrown in jail. The occupation troops would not care if she had a sick baby at home.

Suddenly she felt someone grab her arm and shove the cold, hard muzzle of a gun against her unprotected back. Frightened beyond rational thought, it took her a moment to realize that she recognized the face that was only inches from her own: it was Lieutenant Pomet. "Oh, thanks be to *Gott*, it is you, Lieutenant Pomet!" Karina exhaled shakily. "My little Derek is sick, ouch!" She cried, reeling backward as Lieutenant Pomet slapped her face.

"Be still!" he snarled cruelly, his face contorted with rage. "I have had enough of you ... you snooty upper-class aristocrat! You and your high and mighty attitude—I am sick of it! As if you, a filthy German, were better than me!" Laughing derisively, he continued scornfully, "Well, now, *cherie*, you are going to pay for your insolent behavior!"

Grabbing the front of her cloak, Lieutenant Pomet recoiled his arm to strike her again, but before he could, another soldier grabbed his arm and barked sternly, "Jacques, enough! I will not allow you to strike a woman, even if she is a German!"

The soldier stood glaring at Lieutenant Pomet, who was glinting at Karina with such hatred that Karina knew he would have killed her if the other soldier had not intervened.

Muttering something in French under his breath, Lieutenant Pomet staggered up to Karina and whispered menacingly, "Until next time, *cherie*!"

Karina realized for the first time that Lieutenant Pomet was drunk; his breath reeked of stale beer. Before she had a chance to respond to Lieutenant Pomet's threat, she realized that the other French soldier was speaking to her. Gingerly rubbing her injured cheek she said, "Please, Officer, I beg of you, please let me go. My child is very ill; I am on my way to get the doctor!"

The soldier eyed her suspiciously and said, "Fraulein, I will go with you to the doctor. If you are lying … I will have you arrested!"

Karina sagged with relief. "Then follow me," she cried. "There is not a moment to lose!" With the soldier following her, Karina ran every step of the way, her long hair streaming behind her, and her open cloak flapping in the cold night air. She ran up to Dr. Kimmler's dark, silent house and pounded repeatedly on the heavy door until her insistent knocking was answered by the sleepy butler. "Please hurry," she gasped frantically, "Tell the doctor that Baroness von Kampler's son is very ill! Tell Dr. Kimmler to hurry!" Moments later Dr. Kimmler emerged, his black medical bag in hand, and after hearing Derek's symptoms, he grabbed his coat, and motioned her into his auto. The French occupation soldier waved solemnly to them as they drove slowly away.

Nana met them at the door, frowning worriedly, as the doctor bent to examine Derek.

"We have to get his fever down … get the washtub!" Dr. Kimmler commanded, rolling up his sleeves. "We have to immerse him in cool water until his fever breaks!"

Nana set the galvanized tub on the floor and filled it with pitcher after pitcher of cool water as Karina carefully lowered little Derek into the washtub. They spent the rest of the night taking turns holding and sponging Derek in the cool water, and praying that his fever would break.

Finally, just before dawn, Dr. Kimmler lifted Derek from the washtub and laid him on a towel. Nodding to Karina, he whispered, "The fever has broken; he is sleeping now. When he awakens, give him plenty of liquids to drink but no milk until his stomach settles down a bit. What he will do now is sleep. The poor little *kind* is exhausted!"

"Oh, Dr. Kimmler, thank you for your help," Karina said gratefully, her voice shaking with emotion. The lack of sleep and the horrible scare had reduced her nerves to a frazzled mess, and before she realized what was happening, she found herself sobbing uncontrollably.

"Karina, there, there," Nana soothed, holding the distraught girl in her arms. "Little Derek is going to be fine; the virus has passed through his system."

"I ... I know he is going to be all right," Karina said, but nonetheless shivered involuntarily as she gazed at her sleeping son, "but there is something else bothering me." She gulped and said quietly, "I think little Derek was poisoned. I think it was the milk I used for his cereal at dinnertime."

The words hung in the silent room until the very air they breathed seemed tainted with it. Finally, Dr. Kimmler shrugged, his expression serious. "The symptoms were certainly there. How old was the milk?"

"It was fresh that morning. Little Derek was fine all day," Karina said, "until he woke up during the night." Gazing at her innocent child sleeping peacefully in his crib, she sobbed brokenly, "It was one thing when this happened to me. I reasoned that I could have eaten something ... that maybe it was not Lieutenant Pomet's fault after all, but now that we think little Derek was poisoned and to think how close he came to ..." Her voice trailed off, for she could not finish the sentence. Overcome with grief, she collapsed into a chair and buried her face in her hands.

"Baroness," Dr. Kimmler said gently, "it seems that someone does indeed want you and your son permanently out of the way, and they will keep trying until their goal is accomplished. Whoever is doing this means business."

Karina nodded resolutely as she gingerly touched her tender, bruised cheek. "I know who is doing this ... I am sure it is Lieutenant Pomet." Once again she remembered the look of hatred in his eyes, and the terror she felt when he slapped her. "After what happened this past evening, I have absolutely no doubt in my mind that it is he who is trying to kill us."

"What happened this evening ... are you referring to what happened to little Derek?" Nana questioned, but noticing for the first time the angry bruise on Karina's lovely face, she gasped, "Your face! What happened?"

Karina shrugged helplessly. "It happened when I went to get Dr. Kimmler. I was running as fast as I could when suddenly I was grabbed from behind and a gun poked in my back. I turned to see Lieutenant Pomet standing there. When he recognized me, he was so furious that he struck me in the face. He was drunk, I realized later."

"Meine kind ... what happened then?" Nana cried, "Did you escape?"

"No. If it had not been for another French soldier who intervened, Lieutenant Pomet would have killed me ... I am sure of it." Before anyone could say anything further, Karina continued quietly, "Yes, I know something has to be done. My life has been threatened more than once, but worse still, so has little Derek's. If ... if something were to happen to him too ..." Karina's eyes filled with tears, almost too overcome by her fear to continue. She stood quietly for a moment, deep in thought, and then, squaring her shoulders decisively, she said, "I have made up my mind: I will write to Thaddeus Conterweitis in America informing him that I have given birth to Derek's child, who is heir to Castle Royale. If Thaddeus agrees to love little Derek as his own and allows us to return to Germany on a regular basis, I will go to America and be married."

Chapter 10

"P ERHAPS TODAY I WILL RECEIVE a letter from Thaddeus," Karina said to Nana as she waited anxiously for the postman. It had been several weeks since she had written Thaddeus of her decision, and the wait seemed unbearable.

"*Ach,* I know exactly what Thaddeus will write," Nana confided reassuringly, "and that is to come as soon as possible!"

Hearing familiar footsteps in the hallway, Karina opened the door expectantly, hoping that today her patience would be rewarded. It was. "It's here," she cried in excitement as the postman handed her the letter. Ripping it open with eager fingers, Karina forced herself to sit down and wait until Nana joined her. The room was silent except for the rhythmic ticking of the clock on the fireplace mantle. Listening intently, she whispered," Lieutenant Pomet, he is gone … is he not?"

Nana nodded that he was indeed gone.

With a slightly shaking voice, Karina opened the letter and read:

My dearest Karina,

It is with a song in my heart that I pen this letter. The fact that you and little Derek are coming to America has made me the happiest man alive, and I would like you to leave as soon as possible. To find out that my beloved cousin, Derek, has a son is truly a miracle; and I will do my utmost to be a loving father as well as a good husband. I also agree with you that it will be imperative for us to visit Germany on a regular basis so that little Derek can learn as much as possible about the estate he will someday inherit.

Foremost in my mind at this time, however, is your safety. I urge you to leave Germany at the earliest possible date. Enclosed is a one-way ticket for first-class accommodations on the President Fillmore, which sails from Bremerhaven on 1 January, 1920. By the time you receive this letter, you should have approximately six weeks to prepare for your departure. The voyage will take two weeks; I will be waiting for you in New York. Watch for the Statue of Liberty when you sail into New York harbor; when you see her, you will know that your journey is at an end.

My dearest Karina, once again I urge you to be careful. Do not reveal your travel plans to anyone. The occupation troops are watching for any suspicious activities, and if they learn of your plans, it could make preparations more difficult for you. Just try to be brave awhile longer to assure your safe passage to America, where I can love and protect you both.

Most affectionately,

Thaddeus

Karina was thankful for the silence in the room, as it enabled her to concentrate on the steady, reassuring ticking of the clock and ignore the wild thumping of her heart as the enormity of what she was about to do paralyzed her thoughts.

Nana was the first to speak. *"Meine kind,"* she said gently as she rose stiffly from the armchair and walked over to Karina. "My prayers have been answered by our dearest Jesus in heaven. He has answered them through Thaddeus. He is a wonderful man ... there are none finer. He will love you and take care of you, and he will love little Derek as his own son. With Thad, you will be safe." Glancing furtively around the quiet room she murmured, "But whatever we do, we must not let Lieutenant Pomet learn of our plans!"

Karina agreed numbly. "I must only pack my things after Lieutenant Pomet leaves in the morning. Then we will have Hans move the trunks to my parents' flat, but we will have to be careful to avoid the occupation officer residing there. Once he is gone for the day, we will hide the trunks in my mother's bedroom; she keeps that room locked. She left me a set of keys to check on things while they are away."

Suddenly they heard heavy footsteps coming up the stairs, and the front door opened to reveal the menacing presence of Lieutenant Pomet, who looked at them suspiciously. Eyeing the letter lying in Karina's lap, he pointed to it and snarled, "You two look guilty about something," as he made a quick move to grab the unprotected papers from Karina, who quickly stuffed them into the safety of her blouse.

"Just a letter from Mama," she smiled sweetly, gazing up beguilingly at the irate Frenchman.

"Hmmm," he snorted suspiciously, angry that his attempt to snatch the letter had been thwarted. Turning smartly on his heel, he pointed an accusing finger at Karina. "Just remember that I know everything that goes on in this house, *cherie*, so it would be in your best interest not to try anything."

They sat in silence long after Lieutenant Pomet disappeared into his room, too frightened to speak. They both knew that it had been a close call and one that could have cost Karina her chance for freedom.

Finally Karina whispered worriedly, "If Lieutenant Pomet senses anything amiss, he will have both of us thrown in jail for conspiracy!"

"Do not worry," Nana reassured her, "you and little Derek will be on board that liner on 1 January … of that I give you my word!"

And so the preparations began. They quickly developed a routine, waiting for Lieutenant Pomet to leave in the morning before bringing suitcases into Karina's room. She would then retrieve from under her bed all the items she had assembled the night before and arrange them in the luggage. Her large steamer trunk proved to be a problem, however, as Hans required extra help carrying it down the stairs, into the auto, and to her parents' flat. Before they were able to drag it up the stairs to her parents' flat, they had to make certain that the

French general had left for the day. Even though Karina was certain that he was gone—they had been observing his daily routine—her palms were sweating as she made herself knock. Hearing no noise from within, she unlocked the door and went through the familiar rooms to the locked bedroom where her possessions were stored. All her earthly belongings were stored in that room, soon to embark on a journey into an unknown future. Wishing that she could take something from her parents' flat with her to remind her of them, she knew that she could not. If anything was missing, it might cause the French general to grow suspicious and investigate. She thought of her beautiful china and sterling silverware set in her own flat. Since it was stored in a glass-fronted buffet in the dining room, Karina knew that Lieutenant Pomet would immediately notice its absence if she tried to take any pieces with her. She would just have to make do with what she was able to bring with her.

Even though they had been extremely careful to hide their preparations from Lieutenant Pomet, Karina still sensed him eyeing her suspiciously as she went about her daily activities, and she knew that she was under his constant surveillance. The unrelenting pressure made her jumpy and irritable and unable to eat. As they sat at breakfast one morning, Karina sat quietly, unable to eat any of the oatmeal that Nana placed in front of her.

"Karina, you must eat," Nana said with concern. "You are losing weight."

Lieutenant Pomet glanced up from his food and grimaced in disgust. "Yes, *cherie*, you look dreadful indeed with those ugly dark circles under your eyes. You should see the doctor."

"Yes, perhaps I will," Karina agreed, perking up slightly, valiantly ignoring his attempt to unnerve her. "Perhaps I need a tonic."

"Well, please go soon," Lieutenant Pomet said irritably, throwing his napkin down on the table. "My stomach turns in disgust at the sight of you." He pushed his chair back with a screech and went to his room. Moments later he reappeared, his coat hanging over one arm, as he left the flat, slamming the door behind him.

"*Ach*, that rude, arrogant, insolent Frenchman!" Nana shouted, shaking her fist at the door. "How dare he insult ..."

Karina laid a comforting hand on Nana's arm and smiled. "No, no ... it is all right, really, Nana. In fact, I feel so much better, as if a giant weight has just been lifted off my shoulders because, don't you see ... he has provided me with an alibi!"

"He has?"

"Yes, because now I have an excuse if he follows me and finds me visiting Dr. Kimmler. Little Derek and I must visit the doctor and dentist and receive a clean bill of health before we can be issued a passport, but I was afraid of being followed, so I had not yet seen them. Now I can go with a clear mind, and an alibi if I am followed."

"And once that is finished, all that remains to be done is to wait for your passport."

"Yes, and pray that Lieutenant Pomet does not learn of our plans."

To help keep her mind occupied, Karina threw herself into *Weihnachten* preparations. She started in early December, baking dozens of cookies to string on the *Weihnachtsbaum*, even though they would not set it up until the afternoon of *Heiligabend*. Karina brought little Derek with her wherever she went so that he could watch her everyday activities. Content that he was with his mother, he usually fell asleep.

Karina also wrote a long letter to her parents outlining her plans. They were still in Berlin, but they were to meet her and little Derek in Bremerhaven to say good-bye. Nana was to accompany her to Bremerhaven also. Nana had visited there frequently, so she was able to book accommodations for them at her favorite hotel on the eve of their departure. Karina's parents along with her siblings would meet them there.

Karina also wrote another long letter to Thaddeus, in which she detailed the preparations for the trip and expressed gratitude and excitement at their upcoming voyage. This would be her last letter before she met him in New York.

It was three days before *Weihnachten* when the passports and other official papers arrived in the afternoon post. Shaking off the snow from his wool cape, the postman said, "It looks like we are in for a blizzard, Baroness von Kampler. The snow is coming down so heavily that I could barely see in front of me."

Karina nodded nervously, little lines of worry creasing her smooth brow as she peered out the window. "Oh dear, I do hope that the snow stops soon."

"And I too," the postman agreed, "but bad weather is headed our way. The temperature is dropping fast." Tipping his hat respectfully, the postman left.

Karina went to the window and pulled aside the heavy curtains. The postman was right; blizzard conditions were developing rapidly. A blast of wind rattled the window and whipped the falling snow into a frenzy, totally obscuring the street below.

"*Ach*, we have not had weather like this since the war began," Nana observed as she surveyed the swirling snow. "It is good that we are not leaving yet. We would not be able to get out of the house, let alone make it to Bremerhaven."

"I was thinking the same thoughts," Karina answered, staring helplessly at the blizzard. They would need divine help, Karina knew, so she grabbed Nana's hand, and together they said a quick prayer that the weather would clear. "I can't think of anything better to do than pray," Karina said to Nana, "especially since we are both praying to *Gott*, since he always answers prayers when two or more are gathered in his name."

"*Jah*," Nana agreed, "*Gott* must end this blizzard soon."

The blizzard, however, raged ferociously for three entire days, finally stopping on *Weihnachtsmorgen*. Three feet of new snow blanketed the streets of Aachen, with drifts ranging up to nine feet in unprotected areas. They could only pray that the tracks would be clear enough to travel when they left on 31 December for their trip to Bremerhaven.

They had been under Lieutenant Pomet's constant scrutiny for the past several days as the blizzard kept everyone indoors, and Karina was thankful for the extra *Weihnachten* preparations, which kept them busy in the kitchen. Lieutenant Pomet remained in his room, demanding breakfast in bed every day. He had been drinking heavily. They could not endure his presence much longer.

Karina tried to avoid the French lieutenant as much as possible, retiring to her room in the evenings directly after dinner. But her nervousness grew as the day of departure approached, especially since there was little chance to discuss final details with Nana. Fortunately, her steamer trunk and suitcases were stored safely at her parents' flat.

They were in the kitchen preparing dinner one evening when Karina managed a few whispered words to Nana about the trip. As if sensing something amiss, Lieutenant Pomet marched into the room staring at them distrustfully. He looked from one face to the other and said finally, "You look guilty about something! Just remember that I know everything that goes on here, so do not try anything, and bring me my dinner!"

"I am so tired of him threatening us," Karina whispered furiously, "that I would like to punch him in the nose!"

"*Jah,*" Nana vowed to Karina, "even if Lieutenant Pomet has to kill me in the process, you and little Derek will be on that ocean liner, Karina. Of that I give you my word!"

Their plan was to take the train to Bremerhaven, but hopefully the tracks would be cleared enough to make it in one day. It was 439 kilometers to Bremerhaven, a distance easily covered in seven or eight hours when the weather and tracks were in good condition, but Karina knew nothing of the condition of the tracks—she would not know until they started their journey on the day of departure. Just in case the train tracks were snow-covered, Nana had telegrammed Karina's parents not to be alarmed if they were late. Hans had purchased their tickets a week before their 31 December departure since train travel was limited since the war. Hans had been instructed to meet them at Karina's parents' flat with the auto, but they could not proceed there until Lieutenant Pomet left for the day. Hopefully he would follow his usual routine and leave directly after breakfast.

It was 30 December, and Karina was to leave tomorrow. She learned from the postman that the roads outside Aachen were still heavily drifted, so she knew that their journey would take longer than usual. Lieutenant Pomet had left the flat to run some errands, since he was unable to get out due to the blizzard, so Karina prayed that he would now resume his regular routine. The postman had delivered a surprise ... a package for her from Castle Royale. Inside it was a gift for little Derek, and Karina's eyes glazed over with tears as she realized that the silver drinking cup she found herself admiring had been her beloved's as a child. The elegantly written note that accompanied the gift was from the baroness herself, wishing them a happy *Weihnachten*. Karina was touched, since this was the first communication she had received from the baroness since little Derek's birth. The natural love that the baroness felt for her grandchild must be overcoming the aversion she felt for Karina. Cupping the gift in her palms, Karina knew that this was one last item she must take with her on her trip. She set it on the fireplace mantle for a final admiring glance when she heard a key being fitted into the lock on the door. It was Lieutenant Pomet.

His eyes went immediately to the mantle. "Ah ... what have we here," he said, turning the cup over in his hands. He eyed the silver cup appreciatively. "This is pure silver, *cherie*. It will bring a pretty price on the black market. I will take it."

"No!" Karina cried, aghast. "This is a gift to my son from his grandmother! It was my late husband's as a child! Please ..." she pleaded, "give it back to me!" She made a move to grab it from him, but he gripped her arm in a vise-like grip and pinned her to the rough bricks of the fireplace.

"You want this?" he taunted her, his breath reeking of whisky as he waved the silver cup in front of her face.

"Yes," she whimpered, sobbing softly, "please give it to me, please. It means so much."

"Well, you asked for it," Lieutenant Pomet sneered drunkenly, waving the cup madly in the air.

His shouting brought Nana from the kitchen, and she screamed as she saw what he was about to do, but it was too late.

He struck Karina full in the face with the silver cup, not once but several times as Karina struggled to free herself from his iron grip. He concentrated his beating on her face, almost as if to wipe out her identity … to erase her hated German heritage.

Karina felt the soft cartilage of her nose break as Lieutenant Pomet struck her again, and she felt the warm rush of blood flow from her injured nose. She would have collapsed had it not been for the fact that Lieutenant Pomet still had her pinned to the fireplace.

"Stop! Enough!" Nana screamed, throwing the entire weight of her body onto Lieutenant Pomet's unprotected back. The sudden onslaught caused him to stagger and fall to the floor, losing his grip on Karina. He got up from the floor, muttering in French in his irritation, and staggered drunkenly to his room, the silver cup still in his grip.

"*Meine* Karina!" Nana cried, cradling the injured girl in her lap. "What has he done to you?" She tore off her apron and wadded it under Karina's nose in an effort to staunch the bleeding. "Come," she ordered as she helped Karina get to her feet, "let me help you to your bed so I can dress these wounds."

With a moan, Karina sank gratefully into the soft comfort of her featherbed and cautiously touched the throbbing bruises on her battered face. "Nana ... how ... how do I look?" she asked, wincing in pain as she gingerly felt her nose.

"Well, your nose is broken, and it is very swollen but not dislocated," Nana said, gently swabbing her face with a clean cloth, "and your right eye is swollen shut and turning black and blue, and both cheeks are cut and bruised. You are looking a little better, though, as I wash off all this blood. I will put a splint on your nose to stabilize it, and you must keep a cool cloth on your eye to help reduce the swelling. *Ach du lieber*, Karina, whatever caused this? Lieutenant Pomet acted as if he had gone mad!"

Karina wagged her head slightly in agreement as fresh tears of anger and frustration gathered in her eyes. "Oh, Nana, the baroness sent little Derek a *Weihnachten* gift. A beautiful silver cup that had belonged to my beloved Derek as a child! I had set it on the fireplace mantle to admire it when Lieutenant Pomet came home and took the cup for himself. He wanted to sell it on the black market! I made a motion to grab it, and he pinned me against the fireplace and started to beat me, and he still has the cup!"

"That horrible, despicable man ... I hate him!" Nana cried, "It is a good thing that you are leaving tomorrow, Karina; otherwise, I would kill him!" She looked at the beautiful, battered girl in front of her and at little Derek asleep in his crib and said slowly, "I never realized just how deeply my love and loyalty ran, *meine* Karina, but it is deep enough to kill." Shaken by this realization but nevertheless fiercely protective, Nana got up from her seat on the edge of Karina's bed and tiptoed to the door, which she opened ever so slightly. She had completely forgotten about Lieutenant Pomet's disturbing presence in the flat in her haste to tend to Karina's wounds, but the obnoxious snoring resounding throughout the flat reassured her that he was sound asleep. Tiptoeing back to the bed, she looked at the helpless girl and whispered, "This could not have happened at a worse time ... you are leaving tomorrow! You are in no shape to go anywhere. What are we to do?" Her usually calm and reassuring manner had turned into one of anguish and confusion, and she paced back and forth by Karina's bed, wringing her hands in desperation.

Karina sobbed in frustration as she sought to calm her own mounting doubts that she would be able to leave tomorrow as planned, but as she reached out to the distraught housekeeper, it forced her to squelch her own fears and think clearly. "Nana, there is no turning back now. We must go through with our plans," she said calmly. "I have faith that *Gott* will watch over us and help us with our plans. Thaddeus is expecting me, and my parents are traveling to Bremerhaven to say good-bye, and Hans is ready to take us to the train station. I must go no matter how badly I feel. My life and my son's life depend on it." Quietly she wiped away her tears, flinching as she touched the tender flesh on her disfigured face. "You will help me, won't you? At least," she said, attempting a half-smile, "only one eye is swollen shut, so I am still able to see, and look," she cried, raising both her arms and lifting her legs, "everything else on me works just fine!"

Nana nodded soberly. "*Jah*, you must go. We have no choice but to continue as planned, but Lieutenant Pomet's beating you is unforgivable! And it has made our plans so much, much more difficult."

"Difficult, yes … impossible, no!" Karina replied vehemently.

Once again returning to her role of nurse and protector, Nana sat on the edge of the bed and examined Karina carefully. Finally satisfied that she had done all that could be done, Nana whispered soothingly, "Now try to get some sleep. We must be up early tomorrow, and sleep is now what will help you the most. I will be in early to awaken you."

Karina nodded wearily, already half-asleep.

Karina was awake before the first rays of light gave way to a cold, gray dawn. Despite her weariness, she had been unable to get much sleep during the night due to her injuries and the nervousness and anticipation she felt on the eve of her journey. Little Derek stirred in his crib and whimpered softly, demanding his breakfast. Smiling tenderly, Karina arose to bring him to her bed, but as she sat up, the intense throbbing of her battered face reduced her to tears. Realizing that she must get up, she slowly swung her legs over the edge of the bed and crept around the perimeter of the bed, holding onto the posts for support until she could adjust to the use of only one eye. Finally reaching the crib, she picked up her son and shuffled slowly to the rocker, feeling with one hand for the seat. Satisfied that she was centered, she sank gratefully onto the soft seat, silently berating Lieutenant Pomet for her afflictions. She knew that there was no turning back now. As her mind relived all the past events—her being drugged during the delivery of little Derek; the poisoning of the milk she put in little Derek's cereal, and her brutal beating—Karina knew that their lives were in grave danger.

A gentle tap at the door reminded her that Nana had promised to awaken her, and she called out softly, "Come in, Nana, I am already awake."

"Breakfast will be ready shortly. How are you feeling?" Nana looked at Karina worriedly, eyeing Karina's bruised and swollen face. "Are you ready to face Lieutenant Pomet?"

Karina shivered involuntarily as she realized that she would have to face him one last time. "Would you change little Derek while I get out his clothes, Nana?"

"*Jah*," Nana agreed. "I will get him ready while you wash up and get dressed."

Karina carefully poured water from the pitcher into the washbasin but accidentally splashed some onto the dresser due to her loss of depth perception, since she could only see with one eye. Wringing out a washcloth in the cold water, she gently dabbed at the bruised flesh of her lovely face, recoiling in surprise at the coldness of the water. Quickly she finished her bath, not wishing to see herself in the mirror any more than she had to. She had chosen her wedding suit for her traveling dress, and she prayed that Lieutenant Pomet would not become suspicious at the fineness of her attire. She brushed her teeth and combed her long blonde hair into soft waves around her face, hoping that its thickness would hide some of her bruises. Finally she checked her satchel, making sure that she had their passports and other papers, her first-class ticket to the liner, and money. Hans had the key to her parents' flat. "All is ready, Nana. I am ready to face Lieutenant Pomet."

Nana lifted little Derek into her arms and looked around the room one last time. "Come, let us eat before Lieutenant Pomet becomes suspicious."

In a sudden flash of inspiration, Karina grabbed her woolen robe and threw it on over her clothes, thankful for its high-buttoned primness. She knotted it snugly around her waist, knowing that in her present condition, Lieutenant Pomet would not question her manner of dress.

Lieutenant Pomet was already seated at the dining room table; as she shuffled into the room, his gaze traveled from her robe to her swollen and disfigured features, and his face broke into a malicious grin.

"Ah, *cherie*," he said jovially, motioning for her to be seated, "you are looking particularly lovely this morning with one eye swollen shut, your nose swollen to twice its normal size and bruises of every color. I like the look!"

"And I have you to thank for this!" Karina said heatedly as she settled little Derek into his high chair. She fed him small mouthfuls of cereal, concentrating on his hunger instead of the lack of hers. Her heart was pounding so fiercely that Karina feared she would betray her anxiety by the trembling of her hand, so she forced herself to relax as she toyed dully with her food.

Eyeing her questioningly, Lieutenant Pomet said, "Ah, *cherie*, are you not hungry this morning, or are you tired of eating this slop too?"

"I am not feeling well this morning," Karina countered, growing restless under his scrutiny. Picking up her fork, she forced a bite of food into her mouth. Her feeling of panic was such that she almost gagged as she forced the bite of food down her constricted throat, but somehow she had to appear calm or Lieutenant Pomet might never leave.

Patting her hand in mock sympathy, Lieutenant Pomet snickered loudly, his eyes lit with a menacing glow. "My advice is to rest in bed today, and I will personally check on you when I return this evening!" Winking at her knowingly, he pushed his chair away from the table and left the room.

Waiting until she heard the front door slam, Karina slumped against the back of her chair, wiping tears of relief from her eyes.

Nana came out of the kitchen, wiping her hands on her apron.

"Oh, Nana," Karina whispered fearfully, her gaze flying to the front door. "I thought he would never leave. I was so afraid that Lieutenant Pomet would suspect something and that he would sense my fear and interrogate me further!"

"It was a close call," Nana agreed. She crossed the room and checked the door, making sure that it was locked. "Come, we have not a moment to lose. We must leave quickly before Lieutenant Pomet decides to come back and check up on us!"

Karina hurried to her room and lay little Derek on the bed, quickly dressing him in his snowsuit. Flinging off her woolen robe, she threw it on the chair and sat down, exchanging her slippers for her shoes and galoshes, hooking them quickly. Grabbing her cloak, she threw it on over her suit and fastened her hat, jabbing the pins through her thick hair. Picking up little Derek, she hooked her satchel over her arm and stood one last time in the doorway, surveying her room. Her heart wrenched at the thought of leaving behind the home she had shared with Derek, but her fear of being taken prisoner by Lieutenant Pomet made her hurry.

"Are you ready?" Nana said as she glanced cautiously in the direction of the front door.

Karina nodded. They started down the hallway as Nana motioned for them to leave, her hand on the door handle, when suddenly Karina handed her little Derek and ran back to Lieutenant Pomet's room. Glancing furtively inside, she stood in the doorway, desperately searching with her one eye for the silver cup. She finally spotted it on a bookshelf, and she hurriedly grabbed it, knocking down some books in her haste.

Hearing the commotion, Nana started down the hallway, her face creased with worry. "Are you okay?" she inquired anxiously, and as her gaze fell to the cup, "Lieutenant Pomet will suspect something for sure when he finds that missing!"

"I must take it, Nana, it belonged to Derek!" Karina said desperately. "But should I pick up the books?"

"No! Come … we haven't time," Nana ordered as she held open the door. "Hans is waiting for us at your parents' flat. *I* will deal with Lieutenant Pomet when I get back!"

Nana led the way down the stairs, carrying little Derek while Karina followed closely behind, stumbling in her haste. Stopping at the front door, they both looked up and down the deserted street, praying that they would not see Lieutenant Pomet in the distance. Slowly they made their way the few blocks to her parents' flat, their progress hampered by the snowdrifts, which forced them to walk in sleigh tracks in the middle of the street. But the huge piles of snow proved to be a blessing in disguise, as the drifts hid them from view.

They finally reached the street where Karina's parents lived, and as they turned the corner, Karina sighed with relief. Hans was waiting for them and had the auto already loaded with her belongings.

Hans smiled when he saw them and pointed in the direction of the flat. "The French general left early, so I was able to load your trunks before you arrived." Hans looked at Karina, his eyes widening in shock as he noticed for the first time the condition of her face. "Baroness, you are hurt! Whatever happened?"

"*Ach*, it was that devil, Lieutenant Pomet," Nana said angrily, "he beat her!"

"He should be reported to his superiors for that!" Hans said with disgust. "He is a coward to hit a woman!"

"Hans, how are the train tracks?" Karina asked with concern.

Hans shook his head. "Your journey will be slower than usual. There is some drifting on the tracks. I only hope that the auto can make it as far as the train depot."

"We thought as much," Nana sighed. "We should be leaving then. The train will fill up quickly since it is the only one leaving today for Bremerhaven."

Even though it was only a few blocks to the train depot, the ride took much longer than usual due to the condition of the roads, and by the time they reached the depot, they saw that people were already forming a line in front of the train. Karina watched as Hans struggled to unload her trunks from the auto and drag them to the train, where they were loaded onto a cart and stored in the freight car.

Nana tugged impatiently at Karina's sleeve and pointed to the line of people. "Come, Karina, we must get in line, or we will not get a seat."

Suddenly it was time to leave. Karina looked around desperately for Hans, who was standing off to the side, his hat in his hand. As the line moved slowly forward, she called out, "Hans, I will miss you! *Danke sehr* for all you've done!"

Hans waved his hat in farewell and shouted, "Have a safe trip, Baroness. May *Gott* bless you and keep you safe ... *auf wiedersehen!*"

They inched slowly toward the train and boarded and found seats on the hard wooden benches lining each side. During the war, the trains had been used to transport troops, so hard wooden benches had been installed to replace the seats. Karina now understood why Nana had been adamant that they board as soon as possible as she realized that there were not enough seats for all the passengers. The train filled up quickly; some passengers were forced to stand in the aisles, clinging for dear life to leather hand straps. Finally the conductor boarded, and, as the train blasted its horn and lurched slowly away from the depot, Karina took one last long look at her birthplace and wondered if she would ever see her beloved Aachen again.

Karina suddenly wondered if she was doing the right thing. Turning to Nana she whispered, "I don't know if I can go through with this. I am going to a strange country to marry a man I have never met and do not love. I am leaving my homeland, relatives, and friends! My whole life is here, and I am throwing it all away. Have I lost my senses?"

Nana shook her head emphatically. "*Nein*, do not fret so. You are doing the only thing possible to save not only your son's life but also your own! You are taking your son to a wonderful country that is free of occupation troops, starvation, and bloodshed. Thaddeus will be a wonderful husband and doting father, and you will learn to love him. And remember he promised that you will be visiting regularly once this country settles down from the war."

Karina nodded, wincing as she touched her mangled face. "But why," Karina asked dejectedly, "why did my beloved have to die?"

"Try not to look backward, *meine* Karina," Nana consoled gently, "live for tomorrow. Looking backward is too painful."

"I guess there is no turning back now," Karina confided to Nana awhile later as they watched the snow-encrusted landscape roll slowly by. "Thaddeus is expecting us. He will be waiting for us when we dock in New York harbor, but what are you going to do, Nana? You have to go back to the flat! When Lieutenant Pomet realizes that I am gone, there is no telling what he might do to you!"

"No, do not worry about me, Karina. I know that *Gott* will look after me, and Lieutenant Pomet has no interest in me. When he realizes that he let you slip away right under his nose, he will be so angry with himself that he will not be able to think of anything else!"

"I am not so sure," Karina cautioned. "As we know, Lieutenant Pomet is a vicious man, and he might try and take his anger out on you. Perhaps you could travel back to Berlin with Mama and Papa. There you would be safe, and they would love for you to stay with them." Karina sighed. "I feel better already knowing that I will never see Lieutenant Pomet again!"

The trip took longer than expected due to the condition of the tracks. Heavy snow clung to the dense evergreens lining each side of the tracks, making it seem as if they were traveling through a long white tunnel. Where snow had drifted across the tracks in open areas, the engineer stopped the train so that the tracks could be cleared of the snow. It was slow and arduous work, and all able-bodied male passengers were asked to help shovel snow. Karina shifted her weight on the hard wooden bench and handed little Derek to Nana. Karina was in agony. Her nose throbbed and drained blood; her bruised and swollen right eye drained profusely, and her entire face ached. The train was so overcrowded that she could not stand up or change positions. Little Derek needed to be changed, but there was no room, and it was freezing cold despite the crush of bodies. She was sick of the curious stares and looks of pity directed at her, and prayed fervently for the trip to end.

They finally reached Bremerhaven in total darkness. It was well after the supper hour. The journey had taken thirteen long hours. Thankfully Nana had arranged for a porter to meet them at the train station and transport the luggage to the dock, where it would be loaded onto the *President Fillmore*, the immense ocean liner that would take them to America.

They caught a streetcar to the Hotel Metropol, a luxurious hotel that had been in operation since 1907. Karina sniffed the salt air in appreciation, and, despite her misery and discomfort, she felt a twinge of anticipation.

Karina looked down at little Derek and kissed his downy head softly. "Soon, my son," she whispered tenderly, "you will be meeting your new father. I am told that he is loving and kind and very much like your real father, and I am sure that we will learn to love him very much."

The streetcar stopped in front of the Hotel Metropol, and a doorman dressed in gold and white velvet livery helped them alight, smiling a friendly hello. As they walked into the dimly lit lobby and to the main desk, Karina heard shrieks of joy and turned to see her family rushing toward them.

Frau Winkler shrieked in horror and rushed up to Karina, gently cradling her daughter's injured face in her hands; all conversation ceased as her family looked in horror at Karina's battered face. "*Mein Gott*, what has happened, *meine kind*, your face ... your beautiful face!" Frau Winkler sobbed hysterically. "Please, tell us what happened!"

"Tell me who did this to you," Karina's father growled angrily, "and I will make sure that justice is done!" He looked more closely at the extent of her injuries and said, "We must call a doctor!"

Karina felt herself growing hot with embarrassment as she found herself the center of attention. She stammered nervously, "We ... we had an occupation soldier living with us. He is a French lieutenant. His name is Lieutenant Pomet, and he ... he beat me." As she felt the loving concern of her family enveloping her, she broke into sobs and threw herself into her father's strong arms.

"*Jah*, it was terrible," Nana said soberly. "I had to jump on his back to break his hold on her! This is not the first thing that he has done. We suspect that he tried to poison both Karina and little Derek!"

"His actions will not go unpunished, I promise you that," Rolf Winkler said grimly. "His superiors must be made aware of the situation so that it can be corrected. I will demand that he be removed from your flat and thrown in jail!"

They went to the front desk and checked in, and a bellboy led them to their room.

It was tastefully decorated with a canopy bed and rich carpeting and close to the harbor. Karina looked out the window into the darkness and realized that tomorrow she would be on an immense ocean liner heading for her new life in America.

There was a knock at the door, and it was her father. "Do you wish to go down to the restaurant to have something to eat, Karina? You and Nana and little Derek must be starving."

Karina nodded wearily, "Papa, I am so tired that all I wish to do is lie down, but I am also starving. But I cannot even think of eating until I feed little Derek. The poor little *kind* has had nothing to eat all day, and his diaper is soaked!"

"Then we will leave you for the moment," Herr Winkler said. "Take care of little Derek and tell Nana to call room service. They will bring you something to eat. After that, we can talk."

Karina closed the door and looked around their room, noticing how soft and inviting the canopy bed looked. Setting little Derek on the bed, she removed his snowsuit and quickly changed him as he cooed and pulled on her hair. Removing her cloak, Karina sank gratefully into the cushiony softness of the down comforter as she bent down to unhook her galoshes. Fluffing the pillows up behind her, she settled down to feed little Derek. As the peace and quiet of the charming room soothed her frazzled nerves, Karina felt herself growing drowsy and doubted that she would have the strength to eat. Looking down at her sleeping child, Karina settled him next to her and fell asleep.

Nana looked at mother and son sound asleep and pulled the covers gently over them before leaving the room. She would dine alone with Karina's family. Karina would have to talk to them in the morning.

Karina was up before dawn in anticipation of the trip. Careful not to awaken her son, she slipped out of bed and, shivering in the cold, tiptoed to the window. It was a beautiful, clear winter morning. She watched as the rising sun glinted on the water, transforming each small wave into a glittering diamond of light, a good omen, Karina thought.

Nana stirred restlessly and sat up stiffly, sleepily rubbing her eyes. "You up already?" she asked, yawning. "Probably too nervous to sleep, *jah*?"

"I am," Karina agreed, "but I am also ravenously hungry. Little Derek should be too."

"And I too, even though I dined with your parents last evening," Nana said as she pushed back the covers. "We will dress and meet your family downstairs for breakfast."

Karina basked in the love and attention of her family as they marveled over the perfection of little Derek. The time passed much too quickly and soon it was time to leave for the dock. As they walked the short distance, Karina's mother sniffled, clutching a handkerchief in her hand. "I never thought you would be leaving so quickly!" she said, sobbing. "I will miss you so much!"

"It is for the best," Herr Winkler said soberly, gently patting his wife's hand. "Karina and little Derek's lives are in danger. They will be safe in America."

They found themselves looking up at the most immense ship they had ever seen. It looked like a floating city. They watched, fascinated, as a baby grand piano was hoisted carefully into the air by a crane and deposited on a deck six stories above them.

"The passengers are treated like royalty!" Nana exclaimed in awe.

Karina's father led the way up the gangplank onto the ship, where they were met by a steward. Searching frantically for her satchel, Karina found her ticket and handed it to the steward, who nodded approvingly.

Checking his passenger list, the steward said, "Baroness von Kampler, ah, here you are! You are in first class." Bowing respectfully he said, "Please follow me." He led the way down a long hallway, finally stopping in front of an ornately carved wooden door. Unlocking the door, he stepped inside. Bowing again, he said, "I will leave you now, Baroness, so that you may visit with your guests. We sail in approximately two hours. Please do not hesitate to contact me if you need anything."

Karina looked around the room in awe; it was the parlor and was exquisitely decorated. The walls were painted a soft blue, which perfectly complemented the royal blue oriental rug. There was a blue velvet sofa and matching armchairs, and tiffany lamps on the end tables. Beautiful oil paintings depicting landscape scenes hung on the walls. Down a short hallway and off to the left was the master bedroom. It was also decorated in blue and had an immense mahogany canopy bed, an armoire, dressing table and chair, a small setee and two armchairs upholstered in blue floral velvet, and a small crib for little Derek.

Across the hall from the master bedroom were a bathroom and another smaller bedroom. Karina noticed a beautiful fresh flower arrangement on the dressing table and picked up the small white envelope propped against the vase. She opened the envelope and exclaimed in delight, "Mama … Papa … it's from Thaddeus! He sent me flowers! Listen to what the card says:

My dearest Karina,

These flowers are a reminder of the love I have for you and little Derek, and assurance that you will find peace and happiness at journey's end. I am waiting with eager anticipation to finally meet you. You have made me so happy, Karina.

All my love, Thaddeus."

"*Ach*, how romantic," Frau Winkler whispered, as she nodded approvingly. "Thaddeus is a good man."

"Yes," Karina agreed as she looked again at the note. "He reminds me so much of Derek."

"Well, they are cousins," Nana reminded her gently, "but they were as close as brothers. "Things will work out, *meine* Karina, you just wait and see!"

"Thaddeus sounds like an honorable man," Herr Winkler agreed. "He will make you a good husband."

Feeling better than she had in a long time despite her injuries, Karina suggested, "Come, let us explore the ship. I must learn where everything is at." They peeked into every room they passed and saw the baby grand piano in an elegant first-class sitting room. The liner was distinctly segregated—the first- and second-class passengers occupying the two main decks while third-class and steerage passengers were confined to the lower levels. The *President Fillmore* was magnificently decorated and smelled of fresh flowers and perfume. There were brass handrails, original oil paintings, and tiffany lamps. Beautiful chandeliers decorated almost every room. The elegant first-class dining room was exquisitely furnished with white linen tablecloths, fine china, and sterling silverware. Butlers were already busy setting the tables for lunchtime.

Too soon their tour ended, and the ship's horn sounded a warning blast that it was time for all guests on board to leave. Karina looked at the faces of her loved ones and felt an overpowering wave of homesickness. She had to physically grip the railing to keep from fleeing the ship. Her parents, brother and sisters, and Nana, however, were busy fussing over little Derek so her momentary wave of panic passed unnoticed.

Nana gave little Derek one final kiss and reluctantly handed him to Karina. "Your son will be the darling of the passengers, you just wait and see," Nana said proudly. "You will not have to worry about … Karina, are you ill?"

Karina was still gripping the railing with her free hand, her panic almost beyond control. She knew that little Derek could sense her moods, so she forced herself to relax and bring the situation under control. She looked at her beloved family and said, "I … I just had a severe dose of homesickness because I will miss you all so much!" She felt her eyes tear up, and she began to cry.

Nana put her arms around Karina and said, "If I allowed myself to think for one moment that I would never see either of you again, *ach du lieber*, I would never have told you to go! But I know Thaddeus, and he is a man of his word. He will make sure that all of you return to Germany on a regular basis."

"Have faith, Karina," Herr Winkler said gently, "*Gott* is watching over you. He will bring good out of heartache. He is always with you."

"*Jah*, Karina, we are all praying for you," Frau Winkler said, "and your father is right. *Gott* will bless you and take care of you, I am sure of it. Just look at us," Karina's mother said as she looked tenderly at her husband. "*Gott* has answered my prayers."

One final blast of the horn sounded, and Herr Winkler said sadly, his eyes wet with emotion, "time has passed much too quickly. We must leave." He gathered Karina and little Derek into his arms for a final kiss. "*Auf wiedersehen*, I love you!"

One by one they kissed her, but Karina found herself clinging to Nana the longest, unwilling to part with the elderly housekeeper who had grown so dear to her. She watched until her family descended the gangplank and was lost in the crowd. She joined the other passengers at the railing as they waved good-bye and said a final farewell to their homeland.

Karina walked slowly back to her cabin, feeling lost and alone. Despite her excitement, she was leaving behind everyone and everything she had ever loved, but as she looked down at her precious son she knew that she had no choice. Silently she prayed to Jesus for His protection and blessing.

Karina immediately settled into a daily routine, determined to be on deck as much as possible, as she found the cold, fresh air invigorating. During her excursions with little Derek, she had come to notice an elderly couple who loved to stand by the railing, hand in hand, looking out to sea. The woman reminded her of Nana. As she watched them laugh and talk, she realized with sadness that they could have been her and Derek fifty years from now. As if sensing her sadness, the elderly woman turned and smiled, her kindly eyes resting on Karina's bruised face. Whispering something to her husband, the woman nodded and walked slowly in Karina's direction until she stood next to her at the rail.

"Have you been enjoying the voyage so far?" the elderly woman inquired graciously.

"Oh, yes," Karina exclaimed, eager to share her enthusiasm. "The sea air, it is so fresh and pure."

"Ah yes, there is nothing like salt air, Theodore and I always say. We make this journey to America every year—we have relatives living in Vermont, but this is the first opportunity we have been able to do so since the war."

"Oh, the war," Karina replied dully, "it has changed everything, *jah?*"

"*Jah.*" Cordially extending her right hand, the elderly woman said, "I am Frau Ella Klauka, and this is my husband, Theodore. We are from Dusseldorf, where we own a jewelry store."

Karina took her hand and shook it warmly. "I am Baroness Karina von Kampler, and this is my son, Derek."

"What a beautiful child!" Frau Ella exclaimed. "You and the baron must be very proud."

"We are, that is, I am," Karina stammered in embarrassment. "My husband, the baron, was killed in the war."

"Oh, I am so sorry, Baroness," Frau Ella murmured sympathetically. "Death visited our family also. Our eldest son, Peter, was killed when the war first started. It was a horrible shock … one from which we have still not recovered." Reaching into her coat pocket, she pulled out a handkerchief and dabbed at her moist eyes.

"Everyone seems to have lost a loved one in the war," Karina said as she cuddled little Derek closer to her. "Now I am traveling to America to marry a man I have never met. He and my late husband were cousins."

"You are very brave, Baroness. You, er, have thought this over carefully?"

Karina nodded wearily. "In this matter, I really had no choice. Our lives were in grave danger; a French occupation soldier living with us tried to kill my son and me. See this?" she said, pointing to her bruised face. "This is what he did to me on the eve of our departure."

"Oh, how horrible!" Frau Ella gasped. "He should be reported! We also had an occupation officer residing with us; he was Belgian and no trouble at all aside from the fact that he was our former enemy. He came and went as he pleased. We hardly ever saw him."

"Did he eat meals with you and then complain about the food? And did he watch every move, always threatening to report you to the authorities for the slightest infraction?"

"*Nein!*" Frau Ella replied emphatically. "Your experience was most unusual, Baroness. It is good that you are free of him."

"*Jah*," Karina replied with relief. "But I do not understand his hatred of me. I never will."

"Nor I," Frau Ella agreed. "But, enough of that," she said cheerfully. "Theodore told me to come over and invite you to join us for dinner, Baroness. We would be honored with your presence."

"Thank you so much," Karina said. "I would enjoy your company." They both stared idly out at the placid sea, watching vacantly as the liner glided through the water.

Suddenly Frau Ella nudged Karina and pointed to the west. "A storm is building," she said knowledgeably. "See those dark clouds? Theodore and I have encountered many storms on our voyages. We will be confined to our staterooms for our own safety. Just stay in your room and try to relax, and do not look out the porthole!"

The storm hit during the night, and despite the fact that she had been warned not to look outside, Karina was totally unprepared for the sight that greeted her eyes when she looked out early the next morning. The sea was a mountain of foaming blue-black water with no discernible difference between water and sky. Unable to move, Karina stared petrified as the ship slid down a monstrous wave, shuddering violently as it struggled to clamber up the next steep slope. Moving hurriedly away from the porthole, she staggered across the heaving floor to her bed, where little Derek lay sound asleep. Snuggling down next to him, she whispered, "You and I must get used to this turbulence because we will be traveling back and forth to Germany on a regular basis to visit your estate. And," she continued as her son slept, "let us pray that we do not become seasick!"

The storm shrieked furiously all day, finally abating that evening, with the following morning dawning sunny and beautiful. Confined to the cabin for almost forty-eight hours, Karina bundled little Derek into his snowsuit and hurried on deck to enjoy the cold, frosty air before they were to join the Klaukas at breakfast. Staring at the calm sea, it was hard to imagine the ferocious storm of just hours ago.

As they walked slowly along the deck, Karina saw that a few hardy people had wrapped themselves in woolen blankets and lay in colorful lounge chairs, reading or dozing in the welcome sunshine. Still others enjoyed a game of shuffleboard or chatted with friends.

"Would you care for something warm, Baroness, to ward off the chill?" A friendly deck steward held a silver tray with cups of steaming hot chocolate.

Gratefully accepting the cup, Karina asked, "I have been looking for Herr and Frau Klauka, the lovely elderly couple. Have you seen them?"

The steward thought a moment. "Ah yes, the Klaukas, unfortunately they are confined to their cabin with seasickness. The storm, it made many people ill."

"Oh," Karina said in disappointment. She thought a moment and then said, "In that case, I will take my meals in my cabin. *Danke sehr.*" She had made few other friends; embarrassed, she knew it was due to her appearance. Her lovely face still bore the evidence of Lieutenant Pomet's beating even though she could now see out of her right eye, and she knew that she was the object of much speculation and gossip.

The weather remained clear and cold, but the seas were still choppy, which kept those plagued with seasickness confined to their cabins. Karina continued to dine in the comforting familiarity of her cabin, only leaving to take her daily walks with little Derek. After having had to endure the constant thud of artillery during the war, she welcomed the quiet and made good use of it by reading, dozing, and playing with her son. By the time she saw the Statue of Liberty looming in the distance, she felt refreshed and rested and anxious to meet her future husband. Her appearance had improved dramatically—she guessed that her nightly application of cold compresses had hastened the healing process. Thankfully, Karina could discern no permanent scars except for a fine white line directly above the crease of her right eye.

She was at the railing with little Derek when they sailed into New York harbor, and the passengers cheered and watched fascinated as the massive liner was guided to its berth by several tiny tugboats. As Karina made her way back to the cabin for a final farewell, she felt her confidence fading with the realization that she was alone in a foreign country, where she knew no one and could not even speak English to ask for help if she needed it. Gazing at little Derek, she said seriously, "*Ach,* my fears are returning! What if Thaddeus is not here to meet us? What if he has changed his mind? A fine mess we would be in!"

Her lamentations were interrupted by a knock at the door. "That must be the porter for our luggage," she told little Derek as she opened the door. Turning back to her son, she called over her shoulder, "Our bags are packed; we will be ready in a moment."

"Very good, Baroness von Kampler," replied a deep, cultured voice in response, "and I trust that you enjoyed your voyage?"

"Yes, we did," Karina replied absently as she finished pinning little Derek's diaper. "There, we are ready," she announced, turning for the first time to face the porter. But it was not the porter, Karina realized, blushing deeply as she noticed for the first time the tall, handsome, elegantly dressed and very blond young man who stood before her grinning mischievously.

"Thaddeus?" Karina inquired uncertainly, and then, "Thaddeus, it *is* you!" as she returned his friendly smile.

Crossing the room in giant strides, Thaddeus stood before Karina, his admiring gaze traveling up and down her petite stature. "You are even more beautiful in person, Karina. Welcome to America!" Gently, almost shyly, he took her hand and held it in his own and bowed deeply. "I am so glad that you and little Derek have come to me—you have no idea how glad I am," he confessed. "May I hold Derek?" Gently he cradled the baby in his arms and remarked in wonder, "He looks just like Derek. He is a perfect miniature of his father!"

"*Jah,*" I know," Karina agreed sadly, her luminous brown eyes clouding over with pain. "Derek would have been so proud."

Thaddeus looked at her searchingly, his clear blue eyes darkening with worry, "You have been through so much, Karina, too much for someone so young, but you will find peace and happiness here … more than you could ever have imagined."

Karina looked up at the tall man standing before her and said sincerely, "Yes, I think we will."

Thaddeus looked at the rich furnishings of the luxurious cabin, smiling in delight when he saw the empty vase on the dressing table. "Ah, good, you received the flowers. I wanted you to know that I was thinking of you every moment."

"Oh yes, Thaddeus, the flowers were lovely!" Karina said in appreciation. "I was so happy when I read that they were from you. Thank you!" She walked slowly around the room that had been her home for the last two weeks and was the last link to her homeland and commented, "Thaddeus, this journey has enabled me to rest and heal and focus my attention on my new life."

Thaddeus looked at Karina searchingly, noticing for the first time the faint bruising that still marred her face. "Karina, how ... how did this happen?" he asked, gently touching the bruised areas, "Please, tell me what happened."

Karina shrugged helplessly. "We had a French lieutenant living with us, Lieutenant Pomet. For some reason I do not understand, he hated me. He beat me on the eve of our departure, and I believe that he was also responsible for other mysterious things that happened to me and little Derek. Your invitation to join you in America could have not come at a better time."

"If only I had known," Thaddeus said bitterly.

"There was nothing that you could do, Thaddeus," Karina said softly. "I will not look back."

"I think, Karina, as time passes," Thaddeus said respectfully, "that you will find your sorrow easing and then perhaps you will be able to look back. But we will take it slowly, one day at a time, *jah*? For now, I will tell you about the next phase of your journey. I will tell you a little at a time so as to not overwhelm you, *jah*?" Seeing that Karina agreed, Thaddeus continued, "I have reserved two rooms at the new Commodore Hotel due to the fact that our train does not leave for Illinois until tomorrow afternoon." He smiled. "This will also allow you to regain your 'land legs,' since you have been on a rolling ship for the last two weeks."

"Are the streets in America paved in gold as I've heard?" Karina inquired jokingly.

Thaddeus laughed, a big, booming laugh that made Karina feel warm inside. "Well, you will soon see for yourself. There are plenty of chances to improve one's lot in life, to be sure. This is a land of opportunity for those who are willing to work hard and pursue their dreams."

"As you have done, and which I admire tremendously." Karina took one last reluctant look around the cabin. "Thaddeus," she asked hesitantly. "Do you wish for us to be married this evening? If so,

I must open my trunk and take out my wedding dress before the luggage is transported to the train station."

"*Nein,* Karina, we will wait until we arrive in Wisconsin. This is a joyous occasion that should be shared with friends."

"A good idea, Thaddeus." Karina smiled her approval at the handsome man who was soon to be her husband and decided that their marriage would be a joyous occasion indeed.

Thaddeus led the way from the ship, holding little Derek in his arms as he guided them down the gangplank and onto the crowded wharf. Glancing backward, Karina looked up at the massive liner and spotted Frau Klauka, who raised her hand in a final farewell.

They caught a streetcar to the Commodore Hotel, which was in the heart of Manhattan. As they made their way through the crowded streets, Karina found herself liking this boisterous city. The people were friendly and lively and interested in life. The conductor yelled out their stop, and Thaddeus helped her down the steps to the brick pavement. Greeted by a friendly doorman, Thaddeus escorted her into the beautiful hotel. The lobby was large with white marble floors and sparkling chandeliers. Potted palms were everywhere. Karina gasped with delight when she saw her room, for it was decorated in shades of pink with touches of white and smelled of roses, a gift from Thaddeus. That evening they celebrated their upcoming marriage by dining on lobster and drinking champagne. After dinner, Thaddeus escorted Karina to her room and handed her little Derek.

"Get a good night's rest," Thaddeus advised, "for tomorrow afternoon we leave."

Karina nodded sleepily and said good night. She changed little Derek's diaper and put him in his pajamas and then readied herself for bed. She lay down next to little Derek, carefully cradling him in her arms, and fell asleep even before she could finish her prayers.

"You slept well, *jah?*" Thaddeus inquired at breakfast the following morning, his blue eyes sparkling with vitality.

"I did indeed. I fell asleep and dreamt of you," Karina confided, blushing slightly. She had on a rose-colored satin dress that accentuated the pinkness of her complexion.

"You look lovely, Karina," Thaddeus said admiringly.

"*Danke sehr.* Do we leave soon?" Karina inquired in anticipation of the trip.

"Our checkout time is 11 a.m., so we must get our bags packed so they can be taken across the street to Grand Central Station, where we will take the *20th Century Limited* to Chicago. A red carpet is rolled out for passengers as they board the train in New York and disembark in Chicago at LaSalle Street Station. From there we will take another train to Columbus, Wisconsin. Our home is not far from there."

Our home. Karina found that she liked the sound of those words very much indeed.

Thaddeus had reserved two sleeping compartments aboard the *20th Century Limited.* The beds converted to couches during the daytime, so they were able to visit back and forth. They took their meals in the dining car, where Thaddeus gave her lessons in English as she laughingly recited items from the menu. As they sped through the beautiful countryside toward their destination, Karina allowed herself to relax and become better acquainted with Thaddeus. Although not of noble birth as Derek had been, Thaddeus proved to be just as much a gentleman. His manners were impeccable; his sense of humor was refreshing, and his warmth was genuine. Although she was not yet in love with him, Karina knew that it would not be long before she was.

They arrived in Chicago and changed stations in order to board a Milwaukee Road train which would take them to Columbus. By the time they arrived in Wisconsin, Karina trusted Thaddeus completely and felt eager to begin her new life. Thaddeus told her that his dairy farm was located five miles south of Columbus, which was not far from Madison, the state capitol. The countryside was snow-covered and rolling, and Karina could imagine it being dotted with grazing cattle in warmer weather.

Thaddeus had arranged for his two sleighs to be waiting at the train station. One was for them, and the other was for Karina's luggage. Thaddeus helped her into the sleigh, and Karina settled little Derek on her lap as Thaddeus tucked them in securely under warm buffalo robes. They drove off slowly, Thaddeus expertly guiding the horses around ruts in the road.

"I think you will like the farm, Karina," Thaddeus said as Karina admired the beautiful winter scenery, which reminded her of Germany. "The hours are long and the work is hard, but the results are rewarding."

"Your farm sounds like a wonderful place to raise children," Karina murmured, "and you are doing work you love, which is why you have prospered. You are a very intelligent man, Thaddeus Conterweitis, and I like that." Realizing that she had spoken boldly, she blushed and stammered, "I hope that I did not offend you with my candor. I was used to speaking so with Derek."

Thaddeus reached over and captured Karina's gloved hand in his own. "Please do not apologize," he reassured her earnestly, "for I like women who are confident enough to speak their mind. After all, Karina, marriage should be a partnership—not a dictatorship." Pulling on the reins, he stopped the sleigh and pointed proudly to a hill in the distance. "See those red brick buildings up there? That's the farm!"

"Oh, Thaddeus, it is wonderful!" Karina cried enthusiastically, gazing in awe at the land stretched out before her. "This all belongs to you?"

Thaddeus nodded. "All the land you see in every direction is mine. I own nearly three hundred acres of prime pastureland, and I have approximately thirty head of Holsteins, but that number will increase in the spring with calving season. I supply milk, butter, and cheese to stores, some as far away as Chicago, but people can also buy directly from the farm." Clucking to the horses, Thaddeus guided them up the long winding road and through a grove of oak trees where they followed the driveway until it ended in front of a large, two-story red brick farmhouse. Tying the horses, Thaddeus gathered little Derek into his arms and helped Karina from the sleigh. Motioning for her to go ahead, Thaddeus walked up the steps to the wide wooden porch and held the heavy wooden door open for her.

Nodding graciously, Karina walked slowly into the dim interior and found herself in a large entry hall. Uncertain which way to proceed, she spotted a cheerful fire burning in a massive brick fireplace in the room directly to her right, which, upon entering, she saw was the library. Pausing momentarily to allow her eyes to adjust to the darkness, she walked hesitantly across the polished wood floor to admire Thaddeus's collection of books. Sensing that someone had entered the room, Karina whirled around and said laughingly, "Thaddeus, please tell me these books are not in English!" Her voice trailed off as she stared in shock at the man standing before her, for it was not Thaddeus. It was her deceased husband, Derek. The color drained from her face as she gripped the fireplace mantle for support while moaning brokenly, *"Mein Gott,* please do not treat me so cruelly! My beloved husband is dead! Please, please do not let me be going insane!" She covered her face with her hands, petrified to look at the ghost before her. But suddenly she felt warm, human hands pulling her own away from her face, forcing her to look at the man before her.

She heard a pain-wracked voice whispering over and over again, "Karina, my dearest Karina! It is I, Derek, your beloved husband. I am not dead! Oh, my dearest, I thought that you would never get here—that I would never see you again!" Pulling her roughly to him, Derek crushed her to his chest, his body shaking with bitter sobs as he sought to erase the pain and shock he had caused her all this time.

Karina gently pushed herself away and wonderingly touched the warm, living face of her husband. "Derek," she whispered softly, "is it you? Is it really you? Are you really alive?"

"Yes, it is I," Derek said frantically. "It is I, your loving husband, who has been sick with worry for you all these long, torturous months! When I think of what you have endured because of me, I will never be able to forgive myself!"

But Karina could not rid herself of the pain she had attempted to deny all the months since Derek's death. She had forced herself to accept his death, and her mind would not acknowledge the man standing before her. Derek was dead, her subconscious mind said sternly. Do not accept this cruel dream! She touched his face once more, marveling at how her mind had made him seem so real, so alive. Unable to withstand the mental anguish any longer, she collapsed to the floor in a faint.

Chapter 11

"KARINA, MY DEAREST KARINA, PLEASE speak to me! Please wake up and speak to me! Please tell me that you are okay!"

Karina awoke to find herself lying on a sofa in the library, Thaddeus's concerned face hovering anxiously above her own. He was still holding little Derek, who had sensed the tension and was crying pitifully.

Karina moaned and rubbed the side of her head, which throbbed painfully. I must have bumped it when I fell, she thought dully. Looking up at Thaddeus sadly, she wondered if he would have her committed to an insane asylum. She wondered what they were like in America; they were dark, dismal prisons in Germany. Gazing up at Thaddeus's anxious face, she saw her plans for a happy future slipping away as she confessed miserably, "Thaddeus, we cannot be married. I … I think I am insane. My mind is telling me that I saw Derek, but he is dead, not alive, and he looked so real!"

Thaddeus nodded in agreement, and grasping her hands protectively in his own said, "*Nein*, Karina, we cannot be married, that is true, but it is not because you are insane! It is because you are already married!"

Wrenching her hands away in anger, Karina covered her face and turned away. Sobbing desperately, she said, "How can you be so cruel?" She screamed hysterically, hitting Thaddeus on the chest with her fists. "I am a widow! Derek died in the war! Don't you remember your letter? You begged me to come to America to marry you! Now I am here and you no longer want me! Please," she sobbed, pushing him away, "get away from me. I never want to see you again!"

"Karina," Thaddeus pleaded, cupping her face in his hands so that she had to look into his eyes. "Karina," he repeated again, speaking slowly and deliberately so she would understand every word, "I brought you to America at the insistence of your husband, who was beside himself with worry about you! Yes, I wrote the letters, but it was Derek who dictated every word! Karina, Derek is *alive*—your beloved is here in this room, desperate to speak to you! You were not hallucinating when you saw him earlier. He is real, not a ghost. Please believe me!"

Karina looked at Thaddeus searchingly, staring deeply into his clear blue eyes, where she saw nothing but love, compassion, and concern. She remembered how she had felt when they first met—how he towered over her in the ship's cabin, smiling mischievously, and how she could sense immediately his honesty and goodness. Suddenly she knew that he would not—could not—lie to her, for he was just like her beloved Derek in that his goodness was soul deep. Sighing shakily, she pulled herself up to a sitting position, cautiously rubbing her tender head. Smiling uncertainly, she beckoned for Thaddeus to sit by her and said, "Thaddeus, I know you would never lie to me, so if you say that Derek is alive—I believe you! And if this is true, please bring him to me. I've waited so long!"

He was there in a second, his mouth covering her rapturous face in tortured kisses as she looked adoringly into the dark eyes that only moments ago she had sworn no longer existed.

"Derek," she sobbed, tears of joy streaming down her face, "Oh, my beloved, you are really, truly alive! My dearest Jesus has answered my prayers and raised you from the dead! How many, many nights I prayed that you would come back to me!"

"And I, my beloved Karina," Derek said huskily, struggling to keep his emotions in check. "I was terrified for your safety. I had no choice but to do what I did, but it nearly drove me mad knowing that I was leaving you in that treacherous, war-torn country! The only thought that comforted me was knowing that you were being watched over by Nana and Hans, and your family was nearby."

"*Jah*," Nana and Hans were wonderful," Karina said softly, her brown eyes misting with tears. "They were devoted to me—especially Nana. She always called me '*meine kind*,' and she loved me as her own. I would not be here today, Derek, if it were not for their love and protection." Shyly, she stroked the familiar outline of Derek's handsome face and noticed for the first time how thin he had grown. "Derek," she said in concern, have you been eating properly?" Alarmed, her gaze traveled over the length of his body, her eyes resting in shock on the set of crutches propped carefully against the sofa.

"Derek, what happened … your leg!" Karina gasped in horror, clutching her throat in agony as she realized that his left leg was amputated just below the knee. "Oh, my dearest, sweetest, beloved," she wept in anguish, "your leg, how did this happen?"

Derek looked sadly at Karina's tear-streaked face and kissed her tenderly, settling her protectively in his strong arms. "It is a long, long story," he said tiredly, "and which I have thought of constantly ever since."

"Derek," Thaddeus replied gravely, "was a very sick man when he came to me. He was barely alive. He was hanging onto life by a thread."

"Please, Derek," Karina urged gently, "please, tell me what happened. It is not good to keep your feelings buried inside."

Derek nodded, wrapping his arms tighter around Karina. He looked questioningly at Thaddeus, who nodded for him to continue.

"Tell her, Derek," Thaddeus said. "Karina is right. You must talk about it so that you can heal." He got up from his chair by the fireplace and placed his hand on Derek's shoulder, squeezing it reassuringly. Walking over to the bar, he produced a bottle of brandy and poured himself a glass. "Would you care for some?"

Derek nodded. He accepted the glass and took a few sips, staring thoughtfully at the dark red liquid. "It was at the Second Battle of the Sambre," he said finally. "Our infantry unit was locked in combat with the French for days, both sides taking shelter in trenches, neither side gaining any ground. Apparently the French must have somehow gotten word to their reinforcements, for late one afternoon they unexpectedly swarmed out of their foxholes and charged us. I fought desperately, firing round after round of ammunition, but my gun jammed, and I found myself engaged in hand-to-hand combat. Suddenly, I felt a searing pain across my head and then in my left leg as the world exploded around me." Derek reached down, unconsciously rubbing his missing limb as he relived the agony and pain. "I fell to the ground and lay there stunned, hopelessly trying to clear my senses so I could defend myself, but I opened my eyes and realized that I could not see. I felt something warm and sticky on my face, so I rubbed my sleeve across my eyes and realized that I could not see because my face was covered with blood. I lay still for a moment, attempting to gather my strength, when I sensed someone standing close to me. I squinted my eyes and saw that it was a French soldier, who was muttering something out loud. Thinking that he had shell shock, I formed a plan of attack, but then I overheard his conversation. 'Ah, Fredericka, my bewitching beauty,' he said grandly, 'you thought that I would never find your brother and kill him, but I, Jacques Pomet, always keeps his promises, and to prove it, I will bring you this!'

"With that," Derek continued, imitating his action, "he reached down and ripped my identification tags from my neck. By this time, I was in excruciating pain and slipping in and out of consciousness, but by his actions I knew that he thought me dead."

"But Derek," Karina said, "we had a funeral for you, and there was a body in that casket. How could the *Deutsches Heer* make such a horrible mistake?"

Derek shook his head sadly. "The wounds, the ghastly, disfiguring wounds that many poor soldiers died from … many of the men were unrecognizable. Many times, the only possible way to identify a body was through the identification tags, but many men had lost theirs in battle. And mine," he explained, "what I assume happened to my other identification tag is that when the French soldier jerked my tags off, one landed on the body lying next to me. That poor soldier must have lost his own tags, so they saw my tag lying on the body and assumed it was me."

"But the Army, the *Deutsches Heer*," Karina said, still confused, "did they not have some other form of identification on file for you?"

"Yes," Derek explained patiently, "but many times there is not enough left intact on a body to identify." A shudder ran through Derek's body, and Karina looked up questioningly. "When I was injured," Derek said in remembrance, "I ... I distinctly remember where I fell because none of us had dared go near the hideously injured soldier lying there. He had been shot in the face and probably died instantly, but his head was swollen to three times its normal size, making him unrecognizable. When his body was recovered, the medics saw the tag—my tag—and notified you of my death. They did not even check for any other form of identification because of the tag."

"Derek," Karina asked suddenly, "what ... what name did you say the French soldier called himself?"

"Pomet ... Jacques Pomet ... I will never forget it. He said that Fredericka wanted me ... dead! Oh, *mein Gott*," Derek groaned in anguish, "I knew that she hated me for inheriting the estate, but I never thought she would kill! To think my own sister, my own flesh and blood, would want me dead!"

Karina covered Derek's hand with hers and kissed him. Looking at her beloved, who had endured such horrors, she said, "Derek, there is something I must tell you." Breathing in deeply, she exhaled shakily and said, "I believe that Fredericka tried to have us all murdered! A despicable French lieutenant came to live with us when the occupation troops came to Aachen, and his name was Lieutenant Jacques Pomet!"

Derek gasped. "It had to be the same person!"

"Yes, I am sure of it. But how does he know Fredericka? He is French, and she is German, and he hates the Germans!"

Derek said, "Fredericka went to boarding school in France. She

165

spent several years there, as Mother wished her to learn the culture and language of different countries. Mother wanted Fredericka to marry into royalty, so it was imperative that she receive a well-rounded education. She had many friends in France. Lieutenant Pomet may have been a brother of one of her friends."

"Oh, Derek," Karina said, "Lieutenant Pomet tried to poison me on two occasions, one when I was giving birth! And then, if that was not bad enough," Karina said, "he tried to poison our child!" She buried her face in Derek's sleeve, her slender shoulders heaving with sobs.

"Our child?" Derek said, as he looked in wonder as Thaddeus handed little Derek to Karina.

"Yes," Karina sniffled.

Derek smiled tenderly as he gently picked up the child and placed him in his lap. "Oh, *meine* Karina, what a blessing," Derek said. "You must have conceived our precious son when I was home on leave for Father's funeral."

"Yes, my beloved husband," Karina nodded tenderly as she took Derek's hand in hers. "That is exactly what happened because nine months later our son was born." Karina's dark eyes grew somber as she turned to Derek and said, "When Lieutenant Pomet tried to poison little Derek, this…this is what made me realize that our lives were in mortal danger, and that I must come to America!" Karina shook her head, her eyes wet with tears. "We came so close to death—all of us, Derek," she said, "and all because of Fredericka's greed!"

"I will have her … and him, Jacques Pomet … put away!" Derek vowed bitterly, "so they can never harm us again!"

Karina laughed sardonically, overcome with hatred for the evil woman who had almost destroyed their lives. "At the reading of your will, Derek," she recalled, "after the funeral, when Fredericka learned that I was heir to the estate as well as with child, she flew into a rage, swearing that she would get back at me. I refused to believe her at the time despite a warning from the lawyer, but … she meant every word that she said."

"So," Derek mused, "after Fredericka had me killed, she assumed she would inherit the estate, but then she learned that you were heir as well as with child ... two more innocent victims standing in the way of her inheritance. Then she arranged for her lover, Jacques Pomet, to kill you also."

"Oh, Derek, he was a horrible man! He beat me on the eve of our departure from Aachen, but when he tried to poison our son ..." she could not continue.

Derek looked again at his son nestled in his lap, his eyes misty with tears. "He ... he looks just like me!"

"Nana thought so too," Karina agreed. "He is such a special baby!"

Tenderly Karina placed her hand over Derek's large one as they both caressed their son. "My beloved, you do not know how many times I prayed for this to happen," she confessed. "When you died, I wanted to die also. I did not want to go on living. The miracle of our child growing inside of me—it was this that kept my sanity ... and my prayers to my beloved *Gott*."

"Oh, if only I had known," Derek said miserably, gathering his son and Karina closer, "if only I had known! I was taken prisoner by the French, and I was only at the prison camp a few days when we heard rumors that the war had ended, and all able-bodied soldiers were set free. But my situation was different. My leg was in shreds. Splinters of bone poked out in seven different places, and I was in an agony of pain. I also had a deep flesh wound on my forehead and a concussion. Remember when I told you that I could not see for the blood covering my eyes? I drifted in and out of consciousness for days on end, not sure of where I was. Since I was in a prison camp, the nursing care was poor, and my leg became infected. I lay there helpless, not knowing what to do. I knew that if I did not receive help soon, I would die."

Karina felt her stomach churning and, fearing that she might become ill, she whispered a quick prayer to Jesus for strength. The details of Derek's imprisonment were horrifying, yet something she had to know. If she wanted to help Derek overcome this nightmare,

Karina had to hear him out. Karina felt herself relax, allowing her to squeeze Derek's hand reassuringly, giving him the strength to go on.

"With the end of the war," Derek continued, his pain-filled eyes never leaving Karina's face, "our prison camp was disbanded, with the most seriously injured men transferred to a convent that had been converted to a hospital during the war. The nuns were most compassionate and caring, but the severity of my injuries was beyond their range of skill. There was only one doctor ... to care for three hundred sick men! Since most of the injured were French, British, and American soldiers, their needs came first."

"You were in enemy territory and at their mercy," Thaddeus said.

Derek nodded grimly. "I lay on my cot, day after day, growing weaker ... almost gagging from the stench of my wounds. One nun, Sister Bernadette, spoke German, so we would pray the rosary together every morning, since I had confided to her that I was Catholic. But on one particular morning, I grabbed her hand in desperation and whispered, 'Sister, I am going to die!' I pointed to my leg. "I know that gangrene has set in ... I can smell it! I need surgery, or I will surely die!" Sister Bernadette, a small, dark-haired girl not much older than you, Karina, nodded, her dark eyes large with pity. She was too good a nurse and too devout a nun to lie to me. 'Yes, Captain von Kampler,' she said, examining the wound, 'gangrene has set in. Your leg must be amputated, but not here.' She shrugged helplessly. 'I want to help—I am a nurse—but there is only one doctor and no morphine or antibiotics! We would have to operate without anesthesia; you would feel everything as we sawed through your leg. You would either die from shock or loss of blood—a death I wish on no one!' She looked in concern at my shattered leg. 'But yet, if we do nothing, you will die from infection!'

With her head leaning against Derek's chest, Karina could feel his heart pounding madly, and looking up she saw that his face was wet with sweat. "Derek, do not go on, it is too painful," she pleaded softly.

But Derek shook his head stubbornly and held up his hands. "I must finish." Wiping the perspiration from his sweating brow, he continued. "I looked desperately at Sister Bernadette, pleading with her to not let me die. She looked away, too overwhelmed to answer. But suddenly she turned to me, fresh hope glistening in her dark eyes. 'I have a plan,' she whispered hoarsely, looking furtively about to make sure no one was listening. 'There is an American hospital ship, *The Mercy*, docked in Brest harbor. If I can get you aboard, the doctors will operate on your leg. It is our only hope!'

"'But that is not possible,' I stammered. 'I am *German*! The Americans, the British, and the French, they are the enemy!' 'But you have no choice,' Sister Bernadette insisted tersely. 'If your leg is not amputated, it will poison your entire system! The stench—it is the smell of death! Your leg is nothing but rotting flesh. It must come off!'"

Derek paused and wearily closed his eyes. "I thought of you, Karina, my beloved. Once Fredericka learned of my death, I suspected that she would be after you. I had to get away, to come to your rescue, but ... but I could not!" He shuddered, his shoulders shaking in agony, unable to continue.

"Derek knew that Sister Bernadette was telling the truth," Thaddeus said. "If his leg was not amputated, Derek knew he would die a horrible, agonizing death. But as much as he wanted to, he had no way of returning home. He was in France, and there were no buses or trains; everything was destroyed during the war. The roads were mired in mud and impassable—even for soldiers with two good legs."

"Yes," Derek continued, forcing himself to speak, "so Sister Bernadette smuggled me an American uniform taken from the body of a dead soldier and arranged for my transfer to *The Mercy*, with forged papers, as Lieutenant Peter Martin. Before leaving, I instructed her to send Thaddeus a telegram ... she bribed the telegraph operator, alerting Thaddeus of my situation so he could meet me in New York. I told her to sign the telegram as "D. Peter von Martin." I knew that Thaddeus would figure it out. Finally, along with several American soldiers, I was transferred to *The Mercy*, where doctors amputated my leg." Derek paused, exhausted. "Sister Bernadette—she saved my life."

"And the first thing Lieutenant Martin said to me when I met him in New York," Thaddeus told Karina, "was that we had to send for you—to bring you to America and out of Germany—out of harm's way."

"*Meine* dearest Karina," Derek said tenderly. "I was so worried for your safety!"

"When Derek, uh, Lieutenant Martin, finally arrived in New York," Thaddeus continued, "I was there to meet *The Mercy*, but due to the extent of Derek's injuries, I was told he would have to be transferred to an Army hospital in New York for further care."

"But the Americans—your inability to speak English—did no one suspect anything?" Karina asked, bewildered.

"If they did," Derek said gratefully, "they did not say anything. The doctors never let on. My wounds were so severe that I was wheeled into surgery before we even left France, and after that I was kept sedated for most of the voyage. Once in New York, I was transported by ambulance to the Army hospital with Thaddeus at my side, and he speaks English and is an American citizen."

"And I spoke nothing but English to Derek from then on," Thaddeus said, "and I wrote down on a slip of paper many common English words that he would need, with the German word next to it so he would understand. Our system worked well, eh, Derek?"

Derek chuckled softly, "Yes, I learned quickly, and no one was suspicious of my accent because this wonderful country … it is a land of immigrants!"

"Derek was in the hospital for six months," Thaddeus said, "before he was well enough to travel. We could not reveal that Derek was alive because we knew the mail was still being censored, and we could not take the chance of this news getting into the wrong hands. We did not want any harm to come to you, Karina. No one would recognize my handwriting, so that is why I wrote the letter even though the words were Derek's."

"No wonder, Thaddeus, that I felt like I knew you when I read your letters!" Karina said. "But making a decision ..." she paused as she remembered her turmoil, "I did not know what to do. I would be leaving behind family and friends to marry a man whom I had never met. If it were not for Nana, who kept reassuring me that Thaddeus was a wonderful man and would be a good father to little Derek, and my fervent prayers to Jesus for His guidance; I might not have come."

"It is ironic," Derek said slowly, "but Lieutenant Pomet's death attempts actually saved your life in that they forced you to leave Germany!"

"Look!" Karina cried suddenly, as she retrieved her satchel, pulling out a shiny object. Placing the silver cup in Derek's hands she said, "This was yours when you were little. Your mother sent it to little Derek as a *Weihnachten* gift. But to think it almost did not make it here."

Derek turned the cup over and over in his hands. "I remember seeing this on display in Mother's china cabinet, but how did it almost not make it here?"

"*Ach*, it was Lieutenant Pomet," Karina said. "He caught me admiring it on the fireplace mantle, and he decided that he wanted it for himself, to sell on the black market. I would not let him have it, so he grabbed it from me and beat me with it! He took it away from me and put it in his room, but I retrieved it on the morning of my departure."

"I did notice the bruises on your face," Thaddeus recalled, "when I met you on the boat in New York."

"The bruises were mostly gone by the time I met you," Karina said. "You would not have cared to look at me when it first happened. My nose was broken too."

"Lieutenant Pomet will pay for this," Derek said vehemently. "He will pay dearly for his transgressions! I will make sure that both he and Fredericka are brought to justice!"

"There, there." Karina soothed him hastily, not wanting to cause her beloved any more grief. "My wounds have healed, as you can see, and there is no permanent damage."

Karina looked from Derek to Thaddeus, who was busying himself throwing another log on the fire. So intense had their conversation been that no one had noticed the chill in the air. "Thaddeus," Karina called softly as he turned to face her. "Please," she pleaded, patting the sofa, "come and sit by us."

Thaddeus came immediately, settling his long frame on the cushion next to Karina, his brows raised in question.

"How can we ever thank you?" Karina whispered, her lovely brown eyes once again filling with tears. "How can we ever thank you for what you have done for us? You brought me to America, and you took care of Derek." Her voice trailed off, unable to finish.

"Karina is right," Derek said, his voice husky with emotion as he struggled to stand in an effort to hug Thaddeus. "I will never be able to repay you for what you have done for me … for all of us."

"*Ach*," Thaddeus replied, embarrassed, waving off their thanks. "No repayment is expected—we are family."

"Speaking of family, Thaddeus," Derek inquired curiously, "Did you know of little Derek's birth?"

"Oh, yes, he knew," Karina said quickly, smiling innocently at Thaddeus. "When I wrote Thaddeus that I would marry him, I informed him of little Derek's birth."

"But," Derek said, bewildered. "I read your letter too, but there was no mention of little Derek."

They both looked over at Thaddeus, who blushed and smiled sheepishly. "I … I censored it," he admitted, blushing even more deeply.

"You *what*?" they said in unison.

"I blacked out those parts about little Derek," Thaddeus confessed. "I thought that if you learned of your son's existence, Derek, it would make you even more frantic with worry for their safety, and … and I wanted you to be surprised too!"

"Well," Derek admitted, smiling down at his wife and sleeping son, "I certainly was!" But growing serious, he said, "Whenever I think of Fredericka and her hiring Jacques Pomet to kill us ... she must be brought to justice!"

"I agree, Derek, but that can wait," Karina reminded him lovingly as she gently caressed his thin face. "You are far from well. What you need most now is good food, which I know you are getting; rest, which I will make sure that you get; and plenty of love, which," she said, snuggling closer, "I will make certain that you receive!"

"Karina is right, Derek," Thaddeus said. "You are in no condition to travel. You must rest and heal, for you will need all your strength when you face Fredericka and Lieutenant Pomet!"

"I know," Derek agreed. "As much as I hate to admit it, I am in no condition to travel yet. My stump," he said, wincing in pain as he shifted his position on the sofa, "is not yet healed, and I must learn to walk again—on a wooden leg. I will not limp about on crutches! But," he added, sighing with heartfelt relief, "my prayers have been answered. Our blessed *Gott* has reunited us and given us a beautiful son. Now that I know my family is safe, I plan to take one day at a time and cherish each moment we have together. Life is too short!"

"Yes, my beloved," Karina agreed as she snuggled closer and kissed Derek tenderly. "Even in the depths of my despair, I felt Jesus' loving presence, but sometimes I felt that I could not go on. Because of that, Nana was always reminding me to live for tomorrow in order to make my grief more bearable." Karina paused, smiling radiantly. "But I no longer feel that way. Our blessed, loving *Gott* has resurrected my beloved husband from the dead! Now I want to live for today!"

Bibliography

Berry, Robert. *Germany of the Germans*. New York: Charles Scribner's & Sons, 1914.

Braynard, Frank O., and William H. Miller. *Fifty Famous Liners*. New York: W. W. Norton, 1982.

Brinnin, John Malcome. *The Sway of the Grand Saloon*. New York: Delacorte Press, 1971.

Chicago, Milwaukee, St. Paul and Pacific Railroad - *Wikipedia, The Free Encyclopedia,* Wikimedia Foundation, Inc. 1 March 2013 Web. 2 March 2013. http://en. Wikipedia.org/wiki/Chicago,_ Milwaukee, St. Paul_ and Pacific Railroad

Clairborne, Robert. (1988) *Loose Cannons and Red Herrings. A Book of Lost Metaphors.*New York: Norton..pp. 193. ISBN 0-393-02578-0.

Clark, Sydney. *All the Best in Germany*. New York: Dodd, Mead, 1968.

Columbus (Amtrak Station) - *Wikipedia, The Free Encyclopedia,* Wikimedia Foundation, Inc. 20 Nov 2013. Web. 2 March 2013. http://en.Wikipedia.org/wiki/Columbus_(Amtrak_station)

Gerard, James W. *My Four Years in Germany*. New York: Grosset & Dunlap, 1917.

Grand Hyatt New York. *Wikipedia, The Free Encyclopedia*, Wikimedia Foundation, Inc. 10 Feb 2013. Web. 3 March 2013. http://en.wikipedia.org/wiki/Grand_Hyatt_New York

Hamilton, John C. *Weapons of WWI*. Edina, MN: ABDO Publishing Company, 2004.

Hotel Metropol in Bremerhaven. http://www.metropol-bremerhaven./de/us/index.html

Marshall, S. L. A. *World War I*. New York: American Heritage Press, 1971.

Nunn, Joan. *Fashion Costume 1200–1900*. New York: Schocken Books, 1980.

Purpar, Rolf. *Os Oche Unser Aachen*. Aachen, Germany: Meyer & Meyer Verlag, 1987.

Sidgwick, Mrs. Alfred. *Home Life in Germany*. New York: MacMillan, 1912.

Smith, Harry L. M.D.(in Collaboration with Eckman, James R.). *Memoirs of an Ambulance Company Officer*. Chapter 11. Rochester, MN, The Doomsday Press, 1940.

Terraine, John. *To Win a War; 1918, the Year of Victory*. Garden City, NY: Doubleday, 1981.

United States Navy. *The Dictionary of American Naval Fighting Ships*, vol. 4. Washington, DC: Navy Department, Naval History Division, 1969.

CPSIA information can be obtained at www.ICGtesting.com
Printed in the USA
LVOW06s0843121013

356626LV00001B/3/P